TITLE

**Puppies Eyes**

By Sidra Mohsin

1, Sucking

1, Sucking

I became hopelessly enamored with a kid. I saw his long, dark hair wave in the breeze and it simply occurred. He was new at school and I didn't have a clue about his name however that wasn't going to stop me! He took a gander at me, when his hair was postponing in the breeze and I thought back and I grinned. I trusted my supports didn't put him off. I disdain my supports! My teeth weren't even that abnormal! In any case, mother just let me know whatever the dental specialist said, or the schoolmaster, and she never paid attention to me. She thought I was moronic or something like that. 'Simply stand by!' I generally thought, 'Delay until I finish a book! What sort of sixteen-year-old composes a book huh?' I speculated that if I could compose a book, my mother and the educators and the children at school would at last beginning regarding me! Since they can't do that. They used to let me know this multitude of things. That I dress to scandalous or not skanky enough. That I really want to concentrate on math. That I generally need to concentrate on math despite the fact that I have no craving of turning into a mathematician. Grades! Grades! All they thought often about was grades. They thought it was the flight of stairs to paradise or something like that. Each An is one more certain progression towards God. What a lot of oddballs. Well, I can name more celebrities that made a difference who didn't accomplish something beneficial at school than ones who. Tsssss.

In any case, I was expounding on this kid and I resembled, amazing! Furthermore I don't have any idea why. He just stayed there, isolated. I was reluctant to go around there since I'm bashful and I didn't have the foggiest idea what to say. I chose to contemplate what to say to him all night so the following day, I could say that to him, as though I didn't consider it by any means. Additionally, I needed to choose what to wear when I would address him, this forlorn new kid. He was understanding something. It was excessively far away for me to peruse the title yet it was a truly thick book. I likewise prefer to peruse. I read a wide range of stuff. Particularly analysts. I sort of needed to compose an analyst. Furthermore perhaps I am thinking of one. Perhaps I'm love of some kind investigator. Also love is far more intricate than any homicide intention, correct?

I thought about a wide range of comments that evening, when my mother quit annoying me about math since she rested and the TV wasn't on any longer. Continuously the TV. Don't these individuals realize that they can observe essentially anything on the web these days? When it's all said and done, why allowed some enormous station to choose for you what you should watch when you can simply go to piratebay and download every one of the films and shows you need to see? My mother would have rather not hear it. She said it's burglary, and she didn't raise a cheat. However, i'd much prefer be a criminal than a mathematician!

The principal thing that came into my brain was to inquire as to whether he wanted some organization. Yet, imagine a scenario where he would say no. For sure if he could imagine that I would be the one that really required organization, or that I was welcoming him over to sit with me and my idiotic sweethearts, showing each other pictures of stuff and faces on our telephones? I would be so humiliated if he could come over and sit with us! I pondered for some time why I sat with those young ladies some of the time. I showed them stuff on my telephone, that wasn't exceptionally fascinating and they showed stuff

on their telephones that was even less intriguing. I needed
to discuss opportunity, trust and books and make quips. I
was excessively brilliant for these individuals, excessively
savvy for this idiotic school and this inept town I would
have been stuck in for an additional two years...

'What are you perusing?' I could inquire. Perhaps he might
want to discuss it. However at that point I recollected that
the explanation I quit taking my own books to school was
that I got that idiotic inquiry constantly. I generally said,
'Find it on Goodreads. When I finish it, I may likewise
compose an audit there. Everything looks OK. Kindly
reason me now? I'm attempting to peruse,' and they would
get sort of offended. They even called me a geek more than
once. I would rather avoid that. I'm not a geek. I don't
peruse geek books by the same token. I'm only educated
past the ability of perusing a remark on your Facebook-
selfie. Also most aren't even that educated any longer since
who the screw actually utilizes Facebook?

I didn't have anything to say and nothing to wear, in light of
the fact that my decent green summer-dress was in the
machine obviously and I would have rather not appear as
though the wide range of various young ladies, which I
generally did on the grounds that my mother didn't allow
me to shop without anyone else and I didn't have any cash.
I generally got the sort of garments mother needed me to
wear. Pants. This large number of pants and this large
number of shirts and skirts that fall marginally over my
knees. Sweaters and more sweaters. Nothing truly decent.
Nothing truly extraordinary. I needed to resemble a
genuine lady. I would have rather not resemble some dumb
young person. I'm not an idiotic youngster. I'm a savvy
youngster, and I ought to have the option to dress shrewd.
Yet, the main brilliant thing I had was that dress, that was
great, in light of the fact that my hair is red and my eyes are

blue so green goes all around well with that. Particularly that sort of green. Light. However, I previously wore it to school that day for reasons unknown I can't clarify. Typically I just wore it on events yet that morning I felt that it was vital to look on my best. Like something let me know I planned to see that kid, that I needed to be with, for the remainder of my life, despite the fact that I had never addressed him.

'I like your hair.' - no. 'Are you new here?' - no. 'Hello, I'm Samantha.' - no. Pink sweater/dark pants? Dark sweater/pink skirt? Levis/dim sweater? For what reason DON'T I HAVE MORE DRESSES! I truly needed more dresses.

At long last, I chose to go with the principal thing that struck a chord since that is typically the best thing. Furthermore I considered what shading lipstick would fit best with pink sweater/dark pants. I realized my mother had cherry-red, yet I was anxious about the possibility that that would look to forceful, excessively provocative. Pink lipstick would be excessively silly, and it would sort of be excessively pink that way. I had one sets of high heels yet they were truly awkward and I trusted that he would walk me home and I would have rather not humiliate myself with my dumb high heel walk, since those shoes hurt such a lot of that he may see it and he'll ask what's up with me and afterward I'd need to lie since, in such a case that I'd come clean with him about it it'd be truly off-kilter.

I just chose to wear no lipstick by any stretch of the imagination, and no heels, simply my Nikes, and I additionally concluded that I planned to approach him and say the main thing that would come into my psyche. I was truly apprehensive. I didn't get a lot of rest and I appeared as though outright poo when I remained before the mirror at seven AM. Subsequent to putting on some mascara, a touch of rouge and essentially every surface level with the exception of lipstick, I looked okay, in spite of the fact that it took me around forty minutes.

'You're not going to class like that!' my mother said when she saw me on the sofa with my morning meal oat.

'Why not?' I inquired.

'Since you resemble a whore.'

'Be that as it may, I'm not in any event, wearing any lipstick!' I dissented.

'You actually resemble a whore.'

'Okay, I think I'll just turn into the school whore. Assuming that is the main approach to getting cash for fair looking garments and stuff.'

'Try not to get smart with me youngster! Wash that stuff off your face this moment and don't be behind schedule for school.'

I didn't say anything when I strolled past her yet I gave her a look that was exceptionally furious. I'm truly adept at giving individuals that look. I rehearsed it a ton in the mirror. I recognized some frenzy easily as I gave it to her. It didn't keep going long however it was there, a small part of a second, then, at that point, she returned to her faculties and said: 'You'll get when you're more seasoned.'

'I see now,' I said before the mirror, while I was washing off all that difficult work I did, 'you're a puritan stick in the mud. That is the reason,' and I left the house, hammering the entryway sufficiently difficult for my mother to see it was a hammer however not so difficult to cause her to grumble about it.

The sun was sparkling and I was eager since I was unable to complete my oat and I just had like, five spoons or something to that effect. I didn't have any cash all things considered. I would have rather not go to class any longer. I looked like poo. How are you expected to converse with a kid like that assuming you look like poo? Along these lines, I chose not to go to math however to the grocery store, to take the most skanky cosmetics they had.

I'd taken chocolate previously and that was actually easy. However at that point I was wearing stockings and I could undoubtedly stick them in there without anybody taking note. Presently I wasn't wearing any on the grounds that I needed to show that kid my legs through the openings in my dark pants. My legs are the most awesome aspect of my body. Or then again perhaps my mind. I'd show him my cerebrum later.

I had mascara in my bra, cherry-red lipstick at any rate, some rouge and some eyeshadow. Blue one. I took a gander at the camera point before I stuck it in there, so my back was towards it and they couldn't see it. I'm very great at not being taken note. I recently trusted that I would be great at being seen too that day...

I examined my wallet and I just had two dollars and fifty pennies, so I got some yogurt, since I was as yet eager. The checker kid was taking a gander at me. I think he loved me. I think he knew yet he said nothing since he preferred me.

In school, the classes had effectively begun for a thirty minutes and my math educator generally got irate when you're late so I chose to take that 30 minutes to apply this cosmetics I just took in the restroom.

'Ssst,' I listened to happening to one of the washroom slows down. I was interested with regards to who was in there, fucking or something, so I professed to leave subsequent to cleaning up and sneaked in there once more, without a sound.

'Okay. It's OK Susy. Do a little sniff OK.'

'I don't want to do it off the latrine seat!'

'How about you do it off my dick then, at that point? You will suck it in any case.'

'I don't know Tygo.'

'Come on, I'll do one off your butt as well. It'll be truly hot. Believe me.'

'It's excessively little here. How could I should sit?'

'Simply sit over the latrine biatch.'

'That is awful.'

'No, it's not.'

'I would rather not do it Tygo. Here, take care of business from the key.'

'I want to do it off your butt.'

'If it's not too much trouble. Try not to be such a... how about we simply do this OK.'

'Twist around biatch!'

'Screw you!'

'Screw me? Could I screw you!'

'Tygo don't do that. I'll shout.'

'Assuming you shout, I'll let your folks know that you do cocaine.'

'No, no, no... ! Do you have any idea about who my father is?'

'I know, thus you better twist around the latrine biatch.'

'Okay, take care of business rapidly OK.'

There was a sniffing sound, then, at that point, there was a diminished "Fuck definitely" from Tygo.

'Okay, presently where's my sniffy?'

'Here on my dick biatch. Let me just... ok fuck.'

'God damn it Tygo! You got any more?'

'Simply sniff it off the floor.'

'That is fucking filthy. Also this is your shortcoming! I let you know that you ought to have quite recently utilized the key!'

'It's my fucking coke bitch, and if you want to taste, you sniff it off the fucking floor!'

'Jesus fucking poop Tygo,' Susy said, and there was really sniffing, and there was a 'What's happening with you. Don't fucking... Tygo...' another sniff, and a beat on the entryway, more beating on the entryway, cadenced banging. Susy was saying 'A fuck, Jesus fucking crap... Aw fuck... just, aw fuck, simply don't dive so deep... aw poop... that fucking damages,' and afterward she quit saying anything, she simply kind of surrendered to it, I presume.

It was difficult to zero in on my cosmetics however it was a decent tattle that I could generally use to coerce Tygo or Susy for something. I calculated that I better get some proof so I removed my telephone from my pocket and recorded the fucking.

'Pivot biatch I want to cum in your mouth,' Tygo said.

'I don't need that in my mouth!' Susy grumbled.

'You want to get pregnant biatch? Pivot and suck that dick like you guaranteed.'

There was murmur, and afterward there were sucking commotions. 'Suck it harder,' Tygo said, and rehashed, again and again, until he said 'Fucking sluggish bitch,' and he accomplished something that made her gag and there was one more beat on the entryway, and Susy choked once more.

'Open your mouth. Better believe it, very much like that. Stick your tongue out further, okay, okay, fuck... Better believe it BITCH... fuck... swallow it. No bitch you have to swallow.'

'Release me Tygo!'

'Not until you swallow. It's really great for you.'

There was a gulping commotion. Tygo said, 'Great young lady,' and after two seconds the entryway opened. I squeezed quit recording and put my telephone back in my pocket. They didn't appear to see my telephone.

Susy became white as a sheet when she saw me remaining there, applying my cosmetics as though I didn't hear a thing.

'You inform anybody concerning this I'll kill you, you comprehend?!' Tygo said.

'Regarding what?'

Tygo gestured and he left the washroom. Susy remained before the mirror and cleared some sperm off the side of her mouth. She checked out me and said: 'You resemble a prostitute Samantha,' and she left the restroom. I grinned. Additionally, I concluded that she was correct. I cleaned the majority of the scandalous cosmetics from my face and went outside to sit tight for the following class. Tygo was smoking a cigarette behind one of the trees. I inquired as to whether I could bum one and he gave one to me. He likewise gave me a light, then, at that point, he gave me a look that said, "I need to fuck you" and I gave him a look that said "This ass accompanies a greater sticker price than a sniff of coke you dumb loser"

'Pleasant climate ain't it,' Tygo said.

'Screw you,' I said.

'You know how it is.'

'No doubt.'

'You would tell, will you?'

'I will not. Yet, you need to apologize for compromising me.'

'Alright.'

'In this way, apologize then, at that point.'

'Please accept my apologies.'

'Conciliatory sentiment acknowledged,' I said and I left
Tygo. I was glad to smoke in the daylight. I didn't have a
smoke for a really long time. It's only great to smoke once
in a while, I think.

I checked out my telephone and saw that the following class
was PE, and it would begin shortly. I checked out the sky,
blue, and I just asked why I needed to practice inside a
moronic rec center structure while I could run in the woods
without help from anyone else so I may really partake in the
actual exercise. I fucking detested being sixteen.

On the other hand, I basically loathed everything. Possibly
in light of the fact that everything sucks when you're
sixteen. I would have liked to get rich. Then, at that point,
I'd be finished with this horse crap. At any rate, I went to
PE class and told the instructor I had a cerebral pain
because of PMS however he had conversed with the
substitute fourteen days prior, who I had told a similar
reason. The thing that matters was, that despite the fact
that it didn't actually inconvenience me, I had my period
now so when he called me on it, I yanked out a ridiculous
tampon and swung it before his face. I was pardoned from
exercise center class yet I needed to guarantee I would not
repeat the experience.

I saw them run. I like to run. Yet, I like to run all alone. I'm
quick. Some of the time I saw creatures in the backwoods
where I ran. I generally wished I had a rifle when I saw
them. I needed to chase. That was one reason I needed to
get rich, so I could chase. I used to have a BB-firearm
however they removed it from me when they discovered I
was shooting birds and hares with it. I'm a phenomenal
shot. Furthermore as I took a gander at individuals
running, in a decent square, to get ready for all the fun, I
fantasized with regards to hunting them. I fantasized about

being in the woods some insane rifle, similar to a Vector, that I can run with, and I'm quicker than them and the shot is way quicker than them. I would play with them. Miss them deliberately. Shoot every one of the trees around them. It would be the best thing to see Annabel flee from the slug hail that hits essentially everything with the exception of her thin ass, and afterward a squirrel tumbles down before her, shot in the eye, and she would realize that regardless of how thin that ass of hers is, it ain't going to save her, that nothing will save her, however she continues to run, as she was doing now.

Before all the fun began that I was unable to be important for because of my ridiculous lady's revile, there was a declaration made by the PE educator that I failed to remember the name of.

'Misses Sanchez and Mr Fog can't be at school today, so for anyway has science or history today, we encourage you to utilize the time gainfully and we might want to caution you that these are still school hours and that it is illegal to leave the edge during that time.'

Also I thought today would have been an awful day! I pondered simply going to rests in the daylight for two hours, contemplate what to say to that kid and pay attention to some Motörhead, my cherished band. I don't resemble a fan, since I would rather avoid an excessive amount of dark since I feel that is exhausting and assuming I wear the T-shirt I'd be one of THOSE young ladies and in no time, Motörhead, the best band throughout the entire existence of history of history and even before that will be hailed in a similar manner as we hail the fair alto stone poop of Nirvana which is okay however absolutely not weighty and absolutely not Metal. I truly like weighty metal. I like irate music. I feel furious when I pay attention to music that isn't irate and I feel settled when the music is adequately furious. Pleasant individuals annoy me. That is possibly why I loved that kid. He didn't appear to be extremely great. He just glanced around, with a paper before him, holding that book, wearing weighty shades, possibly taking them off when he gave individuals interesting looks. Dislike a comedian or anything, however like, no doubt... this is me butt sphincters, come and get it. Like a genuine man. Like a kid that can deal with the circumstance. I see these young men generally acting extreme around me. They can't run, they can't battle and they like moronic poop. They talk and talk however at that point some circumstance comes and they all alarm. It doesn't make any difference what the circumstance is. Great, awful or appalling. They need this pussy. In any case, they don't have any idea where the clit is on the pussy. I was at this party once and this person said he was great at satisfying lady physically so I asked him where the clit was and he didn't have the foggiest idea! I let him know he was a pussy and his clit was to be found on his brow, where he had a major red pimple, drifting in an ocean of dermatitis. YAK! I disdain pimples! I cut them open with a sharp blade and afterward I put all the pimple item in there that I can find and furthermore some liquor. Also some salt. The little scars disappear very quickly and the fuckers won't return. Be that as it may, your face will consume. You need to drain. What's more just ladies drain. Genuine bleeders. What's more the thing would we say we are draining for? This bologna here? Nah, assuming I need to drain, I drain for a kid worth draining for. Furthermore that kid... something regarding that kid...

Every one of my kin hunting dreams got exceptionally serious as I saw them jumping over obstacles. Here is the obstacle, you think conquering this snag will carry you nearer to wellbeing. Along these lines, when you are nearly respectable, I shoot, yet I shoot not your head, I shoot your leg, so you tumble down, on my side of the obstacle, and afterward you realize everything is lost. Furthermore I remain over you, and I delay until I see acknowledgment in your eyes. Acknowledge that I am the one. The as it were. The amazing Samantha, and you don't fuck with me! I wished I had more cigarettes.

I had history from Fog arranged straightaway so when rec center class was

'Howdy Sam say you sit alone in exercise center. Do you have PTSD once more? Anything I can do I'm here. I can truly comprehend your concerns so to talk like now or something... '

Indeed those are the sort of morons that are attempting to get into my jeans. He needs to lick my vag clean like a rich twat's poodle. You're so great Ronnie. I was paying attention to Inferno (which is my cherished Motörhead collection) and I considered Lemmy, and how gravely I needed to get screwed by Lemmy. There was this show when I was fourteen-and-3/4, and I figured I could possibly sneak in behind the stage, and get to Lemmy, and afterward Lemmy would screw me harsh, from behind. I stroked off numerous nights to it. I would simply escape and go to the show. Just fifty miles away. I would catch a ride, I would suck dick for a ride. Anything to get to Lemmy. In any case, my mother saw and she called the police and I was gotten by a cop vehicle. That was the first that halted when I stack my thumb in the air, prepared for everything except that. I will have my vengeance on her, for embarrassing me like that! Also now Lemmy is dead.

In any case, here was that kid. He was wearing a suit. Dark shirt, dark tie, dark jeans, dark shoes, and he was checking out a dark watch through his dark shades. His dark hair waved in the late spring breeze over his pale face, he looked to the left, he looked to the right, he drew nearer while he was looking to the right, until he was just fifteen feet away, and afterward he checked out me, and he grinned. I grinned back. He removed his shades and he said something however Lemmy was singing 'Battle! Battle! Battle!' on full volume and I was unable to hear him so I took out the headphones and I expressed 'What?'

'Nothing.'

'You were saying something. I saw you say something.'

'I said something.'

'Then, at that point, what were you talking about?'

'I told you.'

'No, you didn't.'

'Indeed, I did. I let you know I didn't said anything.'

'You're peculiar.'

'Indeed.'

It went so quick. I didn't ponder what I was talking about. I was somewhat confounded. However, positively. I preferred that disarray. I needed him to confound me more.

'What's your name?'

'What's yours?'

'I go by Samantha, presently what's yours?'

'Anything you desire.'

'Okay. I'll call you Stupirandimo then, at that point. You like that?'

'Fine by me,' he said, presently much nearer to me, in light of the fact that with each word that he said, he drew a little nearer. However, we were all the while talking uproariously, as though we were as yet fifteen feet away. He sought the sky briefly, then, at that point, he checked out me once more. Also he said the most brilliant thing:

'I'm Stupirandimo! The ruler of the impeded! The shrewd made an honest effort at school and presently they are trapped in rush hour gridlock in somewhat more costly vehicles. They are shrewd that they don't need to discuss everything except the new show on Netflix, in light of the fact that they previously settled on all the other things. They are so shrewd, they pass on in medical clinics, on each medication with the exception of opium. They are so shrewd they can flourish in subjection. I suppose I'm inept, on the grounds that I can't flourish in bondage. Along these lines, I like that. Also I need to be the lord. Bow for lord Stupirandimo! You want to be my sovereign? My sovereign Stupida?'

I giggled. He sat on the grass went against to me and stuck his hand out. 'Be that as it may, all joking aside,' he said with the most un-genuine face I at any point saw, 'I go by Vincent.'

'Satisfied to meet you Vincent,' I said and I took a gander at him somewhat wicked. In the young lady bunch that I was somewhat important for, they were getting crazy over it. They manically snickered, and they neurotically tapped on their telephones. I got a text from Annabel.

'Try not to get sucked into the matrix,' it said. I showed the text to Vincent and I pointed at Ann, who was sitting in the young lady bunch, with a silly grin on her inept face.

'Would I be able to get that?' Vincent asked and I gave him the telephone. He composed gradually, as though he had never utilized a telephone. He lit a cigarette while he was composing. I restlessly saw his thin fingers contacting the screen, considering what it was that was being composed on it, one letter at that point. After the cigarette had consumed to the channel, and he flicked it away, he hit three more keys and given the telephone back to me.

'How would you send these things?' he inquired.

I checked out the text he made. 'If it's not too much trouble, DIE OF THE MOST PAINFUL HIV RELATED DISEASE YOU CUNT! How THE FUCK Treat KNOW ABOUT FASHION? YOU KNOW HOW EXPENSIVE THIS SHIT IS? Take a gander at YOU IN YOUR H&M BULLSHIT. Also WATCH THE MATRIX YOU DUMB PUDDLE OF RAT VOMIT. DO YOU HAVE DOWN SYNDROME? THE PEOPLE IN THE BLACK DRAW YOU OUT OF THE MATRIX! I COULD STILL COUNT YOUR IQ POINTS ON ONE HAND IF I CHOP ALL MY FINGERS OFF!' I pointed at the button that was send. I saw him press the button.

Then, at that point, I took a gander at Ann. Ann saw her telephone. Her ridiculous grin transformed into a scowl. Then, at that point, into a look that was exceptionally irate towards Vincent and me. Vincent got up and snatched his support, stirring it all over in his grasp, staying his tongue out. Ann turned away. Vincent sat down with me. I saw Ann tap on her telephone quicker than anybody has at any point tapped a telephone.

'These dolts are engaging,' Vincent said and he got a container of pills out of his coat.

'What is that?' I inquired.

'Morphine pills. My dad has a transport load. He wouldn't miss 100.'

'What do they do?'

'They do a wide range of things. You need one?' he asked and he held his palm up with a morphine pill.

'Is it risky?' I inquired.

'Provided that feeling great makes you need to commit suicide,' he said. I took the pill. I felt nothing.

'They kick in with regards to thirty minutes. Very weighty poop. 50 milligrams.'

'Would you be able to like, actually be at school when that occurs?'

'You can. Yet, you would rather not be. You want to get the fuck out of here Sam?'

'Alright Vince,' I said, and I cherished that he called me Sam and I trusted that he additionally adored that I called him Vince. He resembled, the coolest person I at any point saw. Send that to Ann! No one sends that to Ann! Ann was rich and she had a school fellow beau. He was in the football-group or something like that. They did that bologna football-player/team promoter thing with the exception of Ann not having the option to be a team promoter cuz she can't move for poo thus he unloaded her for a young lady that really was a team promoter.

Vincent moved over the fence of the school garden, where we can check out plants with informal IDs on them.

He was on the opposite side of the fence taking a gander at me, and he stuck his arms through the bars, giving me a stage to step on. Furthermore five seconds after the fact, I was on the opposite side of the fence as well, while this large number of helpless suckers were caught in that jail.

'Do you need go to my place?' Vincent inquired.

'Sure,' I said. We were unable to go to mine at any rate in light of the fact that my mother was sitting in front of the TV there as of now, consistently really, aside from supper since that is family-time in which she can guide her dissatisfaction with life towards a few picture that offers something back; me.

'What were you understanding yesterday?' I asked Vince as I followed his fast strides over the walkway.

'Something about mind a medical procedure.'

'Why?' I asked with a sort of frightful articulation that he was unable to have missed.

'Since I need to be a cerebrum specialist.'

'Why?'

'I like minds.'

'Minds!' I said, while claiming to be a zombie. 'I'm VINCENT I LIKE BRAINS! GIVE ME YOUR BRAINS!'

'It's the reason I like you,' he said, and I checked out him, with my arms still in zombie position, and he took of his shades again and he gave me this look with his radiant green eyes and I just neglected to put my arms down. We just remained there.

'You're astonishing,' I said.

'Come on,' he said and I followed him.

'Where are you taking me?'

'To my vehicle.'

'How about you park at the school?'

'I'm apprehensive they'll contact it.'

Three streets away, there was a parking area on which an exceptionally glossy, extremely dull red Lexus was stopped.

'It doesn't look that extravagant,' I said.

'That is on the grounds that you're not looking.'

'I'm looking. You think young ladies remain unaware of vehicles!' I said, while I scarcely knew what a Lexus was and as far as I might be aware this one could cost between 5,000 dollars and 50,000.

'Here,' he said. He got inside and he popped the hood. What I saw was extremely sparkly and there were red and chrome components to it. It resembled an exceptionally strong motor. I looked nearer and professed to know what I was taking a gander at. 'Interesting...' I said.

'What's fascinating?'

'Just, you know... the overall thing.'

'Yeah.... the general thing.... get inside you blockhead.'

'Quiet down!' I said, I was exceptionally offended, generally in light of the fact that he was correct, 'I know things about vehicles!'

'What number of chambers does this one have?'

'Five,' I said. I figured it would be somewhere close to one and ten so I took the center street. Evidently, what I said was truly dumb on the grounds that Vincent was snickering in the driver's seat. He turned the key and the motor turned over thundering uproariously, he hit the gas and I figured my eardrums would pop or something like that. At the point when he let go of the gas, I saw birds fly up.

'Does that seem like it has just five chambers darling?'

I threw the hood down. 'Try not to repeat the experience!' I said as I got in the vehicle.

'It's what you get for discussing poop you don't know anything about.'

'I was simply... I simply needed you to feel that I'm intrigued,' I said, and I asked why I was the one that was saying 'sorry' He nearly burst my eardrums! Horrified me! Furthermore currently I'm saying 'sorry' to him? Does that seem OK by any means?

'I comprehend. You need to imagine an interest. I discovered that from William S Burroughs. In any case, you don't need to imagine an interest with me. It would be silly in any case since I can gaze directly through individuals,' he said as he was driving the vehicle around the bend.

'Who is William S Burroughs?' I inquired.

'A cerebrum specialist,' he said.

He removed a CD from the glove box; a genuine CD out of a genuine CD box, similar to granddad does, and he stuck it in the sound system and this fucking old style music came out. Some lady was singing this load of drama stuff. It resembled she had a vibrating egg up her grab and each time she needed to sing extremely high somebody would press the remote button.

I took a gander at Vincent's fingers on the directing wheel. They were all being lifted exceptionally quick, however one at that point, and each note that was in the show thing appeared to make one of his fingers lift.

'Is this the main music you pay attention to?' I inquired.

'I likewise like quiet.'

'You try to avoid metal?'

'Definitely, certain.'

'You like Motörhead?'

'I don't have any Motörhead CD's in my vehicle.'

'I can simply connect my telephone assuming you have a link.'

'I don't have a telephone, so how could I have a link?'

'You don't have a telephone?!' I asked, confused. The only one I realized that didn't have a telephone was my mother's distant uncle, who had Alzheimer's.

'For what reason is that abnormal? Is that abnormal?'

'Indeed!'

'I don't consider it odd.'

'However, everyone has a telephone!'

'I'm not every person. Thank god I'm not every person. It's difficult to be someone when you're everyone.'

I watched out of the window and I saw that Vincent was driving exceptionally quick. For some odd reason, I wasn't terrified by this by any means. Never did it appear to be that Vincent was losing even a tiny smidgen of command over his driving. It appeared to be practically similar to he knew precisely what every other person out and about planned to do. I pondered what he recently said. How treated simply say? What's more I thought with regards to myself and about my general surroundings, and him and me in this peculiar vehicle and he was so weird and expressed this multitude of unusual things and I just couldn't comprehend that this was going on all the abrupt. I had no clue about where this planned to go. No one appeared to know this kid. He doesn't says anything to anyone and afterward he simply begins conversing with me. I was unable to comprehend. Except if... obviously... possibly he saw something in me that made me unique in relation to everyone and in this way, "somebody". What's more similarly as I was believing that, my telephone vibrated. I checked out it. It was Ronnie.

'Greetings Sam. Heard that fruitcake took your telephone. I'm a dark belt in Karate and I can get it back for you. Simply let me know what happened OK :- -/'

I read the text without holding back to Vincent. He chuckled. I chuckled as well. Then, at that point, I tossed my telephone out of the window. He put his hand on my shoulder, pulling me towards him. I checked out the dashboard, with that large number of meters and lights. There were significantly a larger number of meters and lights in this one than there were in my mother's Spark, who let me drive it just with father who was never home since he was fucking another person.

'Do you have a cigarette?' I asked Vincent. He removed a pack from his pocket, tapped it and got two Marlboros with his lips and in the wake of lighting them both with one of those lighters that open and close, the costly ones (this one had a scull on it), he gave one to me.

'Watch the debris. Ashtray's in the entryways,' he said with a look all over that was more significant than any look I had at any point seen. And keeping in mind that I saw that look, my eyelids turned out to be weighty and I was seeing dark spots. I woke up in his bed.

My head was truly weighty. Be that as it may, it felt better. An excellent weight was over me. I didn't have any worries whatsoever, and it resembled that weight was the weight of joy. It resembled paradise. The bed was so delicate. I needed to remain in that bed for eternity. I couldn't have cared less.

'You smell that?' I heard from the side of the room. It was Vincent, it more likely than not been.

With half-shut eyes, I looked around, and he was foggy, yet I realized it was him. He was a particularly charming little haze! I grinned. It probably been the dopiest grin ever, however that is provocative, 'Smell what?'

'Treats. I'm making treats. Get that sugar up you lightweight!'

'What?'

'You're a lightweight. Stress over it later.'

'What?'

'You had morphine recall?'

'I thought you said it wasn't perilous... '

'Might it be said that you are in peril then, at that point?'

'I... I want to think not.'

'I so expect you as well,' he said and he left the room. Everything was earthy colored wood in the room. There was a little work area, and as my vision developed more keen, I could make out a violin and music paper all over. I sat up in the bed. He had removed my shoes and that was all he had taken off. He might have taken off everything. Perhaps he realized he didn't need to.

When I sat up, that weighty inclination in my mind rose yet I kept awake, to witness what might. I could fall, I'm perched on the gentlest bed of all time!

There was large plate of treats with raisins in them. He sat on the bed close to me and ate one. I ate one as well. Extraordinary treats.

'Grandmother's old formula,' Vincent said.

'It shows.'

'My grandmother couldn't heat anything. It was scorched all the time. In any case, it was an extraordinary formula,' he said and he put one more treat in his mouth. He took his shoes off and set down. I sat up, eating the treats, and I checked out him. He didn't think back. He just gazed up at the roof.

'Great morphine pills,' he said and he shut his eyes. I stroked him through his hair. He didn't react. I got up from the bed with five treats in my grasp. I strolled around the faintly lit room. I would have rather not open the drapes. I felt like the sun would consume me alive assuming I would. Yet, I could in any case see this music paper. I checked out Vincent and I smiled. 'Who's the lightweight now?' I murmured through my teeth.

I chose to provide myself with a little visit through the house. Everything was enormous in this house: there was an extremely huge family room, without a TV, however a chimney where you would anticipate that a TV should be and a colossal piano with a wing. I hit a portion of the keys however I can't play piano and I like instruments were you straightforwardly contact the strings better in any case. I didn't see any steps. The kitchen was not difficult to track down, in light of the fact that I just needed to follow that treat smell. There was a rack of wine, all red, and a major dark ice chest with two entryways and chrome handles. I glimpsed inside. There were containers loaded up with blood. Somewhere around twenty of them. Nothing else. Simply containers of blood...

Froze, I shut the cooler. I strolled once more into the front room and saw I was all the while holding two treats. I whittled down one of the treats. 'This is fucking marvelous,' I said to myself with a full mouth, 'I'm infatuated with a vampire!' and I was pondering his teeth, and assuming he would tear into me, would I become one? What's the arrangement with the garlic? Does he live until the end of time? How old would he say he is? 100? Furthermore wouldn't it be somewhat peculiar for 100 year-old to cherish a sixteen-year-old young lady? However at that point once more, I am Sam.

I examined the book bureau and each and every book (and there were somewhere around 100) was about mind a medical procedure. It truly creeped me out. I was horny. I strolled around some more. I tracked down his washroom. It was bright pink inside. Everything had something pink to it. There was a major tub, dark with a pink edge, and surprisingly the sink was pink. A pink sink, with a straight, older style razor on it and five watches. No toothbrush. I speculated vampires don't need to brush.

I needed to pee all the unexpected and there was no latrine in the restroom, so I searched for it. In the hall, a side entryway showed me a room loaded up with void jugs, papers and a work area. I got one of the papers. There were a wide range of drawings of minds and numbers on it. It said, 'The skank of the future.' I put the paper down and I found a review room, with only a white work area, a PC, a note pad and an over the top expensive looking pen. I took a look in Vincent's note pad, or another person's journal. I thought it was his. It was brimming with numbers and equations, images and compositions in an unusual language that I didn't comprehend. It was a major journal, calfskin bound, and it was brimming with this stuff. I additionally tracked down drawings of young ladies. Loads of young ladies. Exposed young ladies. Some were harmed. Draining asses. I shut the book and proceeded with my latrine journey. I tracked down it, peed, returned to the front room and plunked down on the couch. I really wanted a smoke.

The latrine was the main ordinary room in the house. There didn't be anything surprising with regards to the latrine. I was happy that there was somewhere around one thing that vampires are not finished screwballs in. Vincent was all the while lying unmoving on the bed. I held my hand before his mouth and felt the coldest breath I had at any point felt. I ventured into his inward pocket and tracked down the smokes. Also similarly as I snatched them, Vincent got my wrist. He contorted it and I was constrained down on the bed inside a second.

'Who are you!' Vincent shouted.

'SAM!' I shouted.

He let go. Then, at that point, he said: 'Don't do that.'

'Please accept my apologies,' I said, 'I simply needed a cigarette.'

'Alright, here you go. Have a decent smoke and chill. There's likewise weed in the cabinet under the books. Furthermore don't go anyplace OK. Latrine is the third one the left. That is all you want to know. I'll take you home when I feel like it,' he said and he lay down and shut his eyes once more. I went to the family room and seen as the weed. There was an exceptionally huge sack of it. I wanted to roll. I needed to remove my telephone from my pocket so I could watch an instructional exercise on YouTube however at that point I understood that in some insane fluff, I figured it would be smart to toss that thing out of Vincent's Lexus. Along these lines, I just lit a cigarette and it was extraordinary. I just stayed there and smoked. I smoked five of them, then, at that point, I was finished smoking. My head wasn't so weighty any longer and I was pondering where I was. I opened the drapes of the parlor and I saw only trees, through a glass twofold entryway, prompting a porch. I strolled on the patio. It was high up. Like Vincent resided in a tree-house or something like that. I investigated the railing and I saw that his home was incorporated into a precipice, and that you needed to stroll up a few wooden steps to the patio to go into the house. I thought it was astounding. I saw a bird. Yet, no life other than a bird. And afterward I got terrified.

There were no telephones, I was sixteen, alone with a vampire in no place. Incredible goings Sam. Incredible goings... Am I simply the dumb young lady in the initial scene of each Halloween film? Is it simply that he needs my blood? Do I have great blood? I might have made a run for it. Perhaps I ought to have. In any case, I didn't.

I sat by the little end table on a bamboo woven seat and I recently let that daylight in. I was exhausted. I wasn't exceptionally keen on learning about mind a medical procedure or checking out ravaged young lady drawings. I was somewhat frightened. Who draws that? For what reason do you draw that? What's more the more I mulled over everything, the more I sort of needed to see them once more. Be that as it may, presently Vince had told me not to and I didn't have the foggiest idea how he would treat he would discover. Perhaps he'd need to kill me on the off chance that he would realize I know. I figured I should simply delay until he begins about it. Allow him to emerge from the vampire shut. I took of my top and my bra, I took of everything and I set down on my garments on the wood, to get a decent tan. I figured that to kill me, he would have done that all around except if he jumps at the chance to play with the ask. I'm a perky supplicate. I began singing a tune about it: 'Energetic implore, lively supplicate, how about you play with your perky pray...' it sounded very great. I contemplated turning into an artist. I contemplated becoming well known. I pondered cash. My melody was incredible. I play the guitar so it would turn out incredible if I could begin singing.

'Decent melody,' I heard a yawning voice say and I smelled some exceptionally solid maryjane. It was not quite the same as the stuff they some of the time smoked at parties I'd been to. I didn't actually like the gatherings however I preferred the weed. Furthermore he gave it to me. I enjoyed a puff and hacked extremely hard. Vincent snickered. It resembles he's continuously snickering at me! I needed to kill him. I felt light in the head. It resembled I was sinking. I gave him back the joint. 'For what reason don't we make a little violin and piano part for that melody of yours Sam?' Vincent asked, 'my father and me are very great.'

'Not at the present time,' I said after I put my bra over my eyes to impede the sun.

'Pleasant tits as well,' Vince said, 'I can form a piano piece for your tits as well. I play a decent fun piano.'

'Is that all that you can concoct?'

'I figured it was adequate.'

'It's not,' I said and I lifted my bra so I could check out him. I was terrified to death. His hard dick was looming over my eyes.

'I doesn't nibble,' Vince said.

'In any case, possibly I do,' I said and I digit on my teeth. Fearsome Sam. Then, at that point, I kissed his dick. He had a major dick. You check out him and you don't anticipate a major dick. Furthermore it was so pale. So enormous and pale. I gave it another kiss. Then, at that point, I gave it a lick. And afterward he pushed my head down on the sweater I was lying on, and he constrained that whole thing down my throat. I had tears in my eyes.

'It improves with training,' Vince said. I was unable to say or do anything. Also I would have rather not chomp. I felt like I was suffocating. I was unable to relax. And afterward he removed it from there. I took a full breath. Only one fucking breath. And afterward he put that thing back in there. All over, more quick and fast. An ever increasing number of tears in my eyes. I was unable to take it any longer. What's more exactly when I was nearly attempting to drive him away, of breaking the deadens I appeared to have, he gradually moved his dick out of my mouth, and I thought it was finished, however at that point he repeated the experience, for multiple times, and abruptly there was his face, extremely near my face and he held my lips between his thumb and forefinger and he said: 'We haven't kissed. Also you must bite a piece on a game life before I'm going to,' and afterward he sat over my midsection, jolted of and came all around my tits. He was spreading the sperm over my tits. I let him. I chuckled. I needed to kiss him. I was irate that he would have rather not kiss me. It was his own dick! Also since dick was being pressed void and being scoured clean with my areolas. It sure was something.

'Kiss me you butt sphincter!' I said. His reaction to that was holding a pack of game life extra solid before me. Furthermore I could barely handle it. Am I not Sam? I took one goddamn it! I took one...

'Come on, how about we scrub down,' he said and he adhered his hand out to me. He pulled me up starting from the earliest stage. He saw everything. I just saw his dick and balls. He was strolling with me to the washroom with his hand behind me. With his other hand he slackened his tie.

'You're the best thing Sammie,' he said. I tried to avoid that he called me Sammie. I needed him to call me Sam.

'I think Dracula is the one that should suck Vince,' I said. I didn't have the foggiest idea what came over me. He lifted up my exposed body by the abdomen and pushed me against the divider with mind blowing power.

'How the screw treated simply say?!'

'It was only a joke Vince...' I murmured in complete dread.

He moved his pale face near mine, checked out me with this piercing look of vegetation and I withered.

'It's serious stuff,' he said, 'a joke should be interesting.'

Am I Sam? I pondered briefly. Am I still Sam? Also I concluded that I was still Sam. Sam I am. Furthermore along these lines, I said: 'It is pretty mind-blowingly amusing Vince. Don't you get it?'

He put me down and he kissed me. 'I love you,' he said.

2, Ghost

2, Ghost

He washed me under the shower and gave me a robe, a pink one. He was butt stripped, partaking in that weed, moving to Thin Lizzy, that appeared to appear unexpectedly. I didn't see any speakers until I began checking out the roof. Furthermore the woofers probably been incorporated into the floor or something, since it was vibrating a bit. He moved a joint for me as well, and not one of those truly impressive ones that he gave me before yet a milder one. I needed to return home sooner or later. Return into that. What's more they will pass judgment on me for leaving their idiotic little air pocket, regardless of whether it was uniquely for one evening.

I preferred his moving. It was for the most part sluggish. In any case, his fingers did all kind of quick stuff. It was somewhat bizarre. I didn't feel similar as moving. I was worn out and weighty. In any case, I felt pleasant, and he didn't request that I join. I was simply sitting on that couch and I watched him dance.

'You look significantly better stripped then you did when you were dressed today you know,' Vincent said.

'Much obliged.'

'It's anything but a supplement.'

'Same difference either way.'

'It implies you dress crappy.'

'Better believe it, I have nothing to wear.'

'We should go out to shop then, at that point. Or on the other hand we could go do the...' (he checked out the clock on the divider) '...half hour of school that is left. To do that.'

I grinned more extensive than I had grinned since I shot my first bunny in the eye at age ten. 'You will take me shopping!' I shouted.

'Loosen up OK, how about we have espresso first. Long ride.'

'How treat mean long ride? How a long way from town do you live?'

'30 minutes. However, you can't shop around.'

'Then, at that point, where would you like to shop? As far as possible in fucking Denver?'

'New York.'

'You're joking right?'

'I have great espresso,' he said and he left me with the music: Romeo and the forlorn young lady. I cried. I just stayed there and I cried. I was unable to help it. I continued to cry. I trusted he wouldn't see it, however at that point once more, I sort of wished he did.

I got wearing my idiotic garments on the porch and strolled back in the room. 'Where are you?!' I shouted when I went into the vacant room.

'Here Sammie,' Vincent said. It came from the room. I strolled in and Vince was getting into a white suit before an enormous mirror and I could simply see him in it. Everything was white with the exception of the tie, which was dark. I assisted him with getting the collar right.

'Espresso will be prepared in five,' he said and he left the room. I examined that mirror. I envisioned myself wearing a wide range of stuff that I planned to purchase in NYC. This was unrealistic. What's more I understood that. What's more I said it to the mirror. 'It's unrealistic Sam. So it's false,' and I contemplated that for a brief period and afterward I thought: 'However on the off chance that it's just somewhat evident, that is adequate for me,' and I got the plate of treats that was as yet on the bed, ate one and took the rest to the front room, that Vincent was simply entering, putting a silver watch over his wrist. He strolled into the kitchen and returned with two cappuccinos that appeared as though they were imported straight out of Venice. It was incredible espresso. Basically he was correct with regards to that.

As we were strolling down the steps outside of his home, I was actually very astonished.

'Did you convey me up this large number of steps?'

'Indeed.'

'I would rather not affront you however you don't look so solid.'

'You're not offending me. It's way better to be much more grounded than you look then the reverse way around.'

'I suppose you're correct.'

There was a little carport on the lower part of the steps. In that carport was the Lexus. Furthermore Vince drove it over the rock gradually.

'Would you be able to go any quicker?'

'You would rather not annoyed the backwoods. This backwoods is sacred.'

'In what manner or capacity?'

'Since I live in it.'

'Anyway, assuming you would live in a dumpster, the dumpster would be sacred as well?'

'This planet is the dumpster of the universe however it is likewise the most heavenly of all.'

'Amazing,' I said. I was getting somewhat burnt out on this. For what reason would he be able to simply make a typical discussion about nothing? For what reason did it generally need to be profound philosophical thing of some kind?

'I get it Vince, you're exceptionally profound,' I said after a delay that was excessively long.

'Not quite as profound as you,' he said, as he scoured the rear of his pointer over my throat.

I recently moaned. I didn't have the foggiest idea what else to do. Vince opened the window and lit a cigarette.

'You have any guardians?' he inquired.

'I don't want to discuss my folks,' I said.

'I simply needed to know whether or not they exist. There's nothing more to it. We need to go let your folks know that you are disappearing for some time.'

'No. They won't let me. However, I couldn't care less. I don't care a lot! You don't have any acquaintance with me. I'm fucking Sam!'

'Better believe it, that is extraordinary and everything except assuming I simply take you, there will be an examination, they'll connect me to you since they saw you last with me, they'll filter tags and there exceeds all expectations. I'm no pussy either but on the other hand I'm no imbecile. How about we go to your folks first huh? In the event that you wouldn't have tossed your telephone out of the window you wouldn't have this issue possibly?'

'Yet, you disdain telephones!'

'I didn't say that.'

'However at that point, how about you have one?'

'Since I needn't bother with one. Be that as it may, you do.'

I watched out of the window. We were driving out of the woods towards town. I had seen this street previously, when me and my father went setting up camp. We went setting up camp some of the time. Some of the time he came and took me setting up camp. I needed to go in that street. I said nothing. I recalled that street.

'Where do you live?' Vincent asked, as he was tossing his cigarette out of the window.

'Try not to go to my folks Vince.'

'Don't Vince me child. You want to go out on the town to shop, you need to tell.'

'However, they won't release me!'

'They will.'

'Vince, you don't have the foggiest idea about my mother.'

'I know everyone. Believe me.'

'Vince...'

'What have I recently educated you regarding the Vincing! Quit Vincing me. I'll do the Vincing around here! I'll Vince us anyplace and when you cross paths with Vince, I will

Vince our method of it! I'm the Vincinator! Presently where the fuck do they reside Sam?!'

'Second road on the left... Vincinator.'

'Alright. Which one is it?'

'Third on the right.'

'This one?'

'Indeed. That one.'

'Remain in the vehicle.'

'What?!'

'Remain in the vehicle.'

'What are you going to do?'

'Remain in the vehicle.'

'Are you going to...' I said and afterward he pummeled the entryway. I watched him approach the house. I saw him ring the ringer. My mom opened. He was offering something to her. She looked extremely upset with regards to what he was talking about. She let him into the house. He had left his cigarette pack on the dashboard. I took one. I smoked. I was exceptionally anxious. I believed that possibly Vincent would kill her. I sort of needed him to kill her. However at that point I didn't need him to kill her. I didn't need her to pass on. I simply needed her to disappear. After I smoked the last cigarette of the pack, he came out. He strolled nonchalantly to the vehicle. My mother opened the entryway.

'You can't do this!' I heard. I opened the window a little.

'You'd be stunned of what I can do.'

'That is my youngster!'

'An offspring of God, preeminent.'

'However... but...'

'I need to go woman. Kindly reason me.'

'However... but...' my mother said to Vincent's back. He got into the vehicle and drove off.

'How did you respond?' I asked with wide eyes.

'An enchanted stunt,' he said.

'What? WHAT? What the fuck would you say you are referring to Vince?! You say a lot of fucking poo I can't fucking comprehend you Vince YOU NEED TO TELL ME WHAT YOU DID!'

He turned away from me, at the traffic and said, 'I'll tell you on the roadway. Where's my cigarettes?'

'I smoked them.'

'Then, at that point, we better go get some more right?'

'You need to counterfeit ID?'

'I have everything.'

'What did you do Vince?'

'Try not to stress over it. Nothing. Here is a corner store. For what reason do I live here? I became weary of New York, went to LA, back to New York, Denmark for some time and afterward I simply needed something calm so I wound up here with my father yet crap... what a lot of exhausting hogwash. Everything is exhausting babble. You want to top her off? You realize which gas to utilize, right?'

'No.'

'Ordinary.'

'Alright.'

We escaped the vehicle. I got the standard gas. He opened the tank. I felt cool since he was going into the service station and I was topping off his vehicle.

'You need anything more? A cola or something?' he shouted before he entered.

'7 up!' I shouted and he put his thumb in the air. I heard a tick. I surmise that implied the tank was full. I shut it and plunked down on the hood. Vincent left with two seven ups and gave one to me. We got in and he drove off. He gave me a cigarette. It was magnificent.

'Is it true that you are truly going to drive the entire way to New York?'

'Indeed, in three days, we'll be there.'

'Is it true or not that you will drive for multi day's in a row?'

'No.'

'Alright. However, how treats father do? How would you bear the cost of this? What's more how have you managed my mother?'

'Try not to stress over it. Try not to stress over it. What's more don't stress over it.'

'You need to tell me or I need to get out.'

Vince halted along the edge of the street and opened the entryway, 'alright,' he said.

'Simply let me know Vince.'

'On the roadway.'

I murmured. I didn't have any idea what to think. I needed
to know what he did NOW. I HAD to know. 'Simply let me
know now,' I said.

He escaped the vehicle, strolled around and hunched down
before me. 'Mind a medical procedure,' he said.

'What?!'

'I brained a medical procedure.'

I escaped the vehicle. 'VINCE I CAN'T STAND THIS
ANYMORE! YOU HAVE TO TELL ME WHAT YOU DID OR
I'M GONNA WALK!' I hollered.

A red truck halted behind us. It was Ronnie's truck. Ronnie
got out.

'SAM!' he shouted, 'What's happening here?!'

'It's not your issue to worry about blondie,' Vincent said.

'You avoid her!' Ronnie said, 'Come on Sam. I'll take you
home to your mother.'

I checked out Vince. He lifted his shoulders and spread his
arms. There was a contrite grin all over. Ronnie approached
me and he put his arm behind me. 'What are you doing
Sam?' he asked, 'This creep didn't hurt you, did he?'

'He didn't,' I said as I strolled with Ronnie to his truck. I
took a gander at Vincent. I needed him to accomplish

something. I needed to go to New York. I needed to say something. I got in Ronnie's truck.

'Sam. Tune in. Assuming that he hurt you, I need to know.'

'He didn't hurt me Ron.'

'You guarantee?'

'I guarantee he didn't hurt me.'

'Alright,' Ronnie said and he turned the vehicle around over the street. Following twenty seconds Vincent came flying by in his Lexus. He shot past us like a rocket in that vehicle. 'Butt sphincter! YOU WANNA DIE!' Ronnie shouted in alarm.

'He can't hear you Ronnie.'

'If you don't mind, kindly call me Ron. Also how were you doing that crawl?'

'He's not a killjoy.'

'He resembles a jerk to me.'

'I like him.'

'No, you don't.'

'I do. Furthermore be great or I'm escaping your dumb truck.'

Ronnie was quiet after I said that. At the point when he dropped me off at home, I saw that he needed to say something. He nearly said it, however he didn't and afterward he drove away.

I went into the house. My mother was coming towards me. She had been crying. 'SAM!' she shouted in complete craziness. 'O my God Sam! I thought... What in the name of...? Who is that kid?'

'That is Vincent,' I said.

She held my face with two hands. 'He's Satan Sam! That kid is Satan!' and afterward she plunked down on the couch and covered her face in her grasp. I sat close to her. I didn't contact her.

'How did he respond?' I inquired.

'He... he... he got defensive!' she replied.

'His teeth?'

'He said you knew.'

'Knew what?'

'That he is... that he is... perhaps better on the off chance that you don't have the foggiest idea.'

'A vampire?' I asked and my mother broke into one more spasm of mania.

'Did he... did he turn you?'

'He didn't.'

'Say thanks to God! I thought... I thought all the time... Sam you need to avoid that kid... you need to guarantee me Sam!'

'I'm going to my room,' I said.

'If it's not too much trouble, guarantee me Sam!'

'I'M GOING TO MY FUCKING ROOM!' I shouted at the highest point of my aches. My mother began crying once more. I went to my room and took a seat at my work area. I needed another cigarette. I needed to go for a run. I just put my head on my interweaved fingers that I set on the work area. I wanted to shout. 'Jesus fucking Christ,' I murmured, and I stayed there like that for somewhere around five minutes before I heard a thump on the entryway.

'Darling would I be able to come ready? We need to discuss that...'

'Disappear I would rather not talk at the present time!'

'In any case, honey. I...'

'Kindly disappear.'

'In any case, you need to guarantee me first that whatever you do...'

'Kindly GO AWAY!' I hollered.

'I will converse with your dad. He'll be home soon. I don't have any idea what... it's so abnormal.'

'Disappear,' I said and she disappeared. I set down on the bed. I was examining my pocket for my telephone. Obviously, I didn't track down my telephone. I tracked down a piece of paper.

Say the following words multiple times and afterward multiple times the name of the phantom you need to gather: 'Hadi-moso, hadi-moso, gommaexcrantorus di" Doesn't work with exhausting individuals. They have no phantom. Be that as it may, for what reason would need to bring an exhausting phantom in any case?

Love Vince.

P.S. you can do it once so consider it cautiously.

'Jesus fucking Christ Vince,' I said, and afterward I said 'Hadi-moso, hadi-moso, gommaexrantorus di,' multiple times, each time somewhat stronger, and afterward I said: 'Lemmy Kilmister, Lemmy Kilmister, Lemmy Kilmister,' and exactly when I said that, it began coming down hard, and there was thunder. Three strucks of thunder were heard and with the third dumbfounded, I heard an intensely misshaped low pitch guitar and a picture started to arise in the divider, more clear and more clear, until I saw his face. It was him. It was Lemmy.

'Good tidings from the opposite side sweetheart,' he said in his amazing voice.

'Lemmy?'

'Just his phantom. I was hoping to get gathered sometime at this point. And afterward I get brought by an easily overlooked detail like you. I forever was a knave. Be that as it may, it took some time before I turned into a tricky son of a gun. How treat need honey? You want to signature?'

'O. M. G. indeed! Kindly sign my tit!'

'Okay, let me simply escape the divider first.'

Step by step, Lemmy loosened up from the divider, and became three-layered. It resembled he never passed on. However at that point again, he won't ever do. He remained there for a couple of moments, after he loosened up from the divider. He stood firmer than any man I'd at any point seen, even in films or works of art. He lit a smoke, checked out me and smiled. I shuddered.

'We should check whether I have my pen, observing your pen is the hardest thing about thinking of you know. How about you take your top of while I do that so we can get to business eh sweetheart? How old would you say you are in any case?'

'Eighteen.'

'Try not to deceive me sweetheart, ain't no fucking point in any case cuz how are you going to sue an apparition? Contemplate that.'

'I'm seventeen,' I said. He grinned and got a pen out of one of the many pockets of his tore jean coat.

'What's your name sweetheart?'

'Sammie.'

'Okay. Here is something great; "Sweet Sammie, you have my true commendations with respect to your peppy tits. - Lemmy Kilmister." and that will be on there everlastingly and no one but you can see it and everybody that gets a piece of that ass huh... ain't that a provocative revile?'

I checked out my tits in the mirror. He had the most wonderful penmanship and such an intricate and elaborate signature. I found in the mirror that Lemmy was putting his hands on me. I heard him murmur in my ear: 'You at any point got screwed by an apparition sweetheart?'

3, Forty

Ronnie strolled in with yellow Tulips and a grin. He plunked down on a seat close to my bed. 'They said you were resting. I said I needed to see you in any case and I vowed not to awaken you so they let me in. In any case, you were at that point alert, presently would you say you weren't?'

'Sort of,' I said.

'How are you?'

'Is it true that i was dead?'

'That is amusing. They said you were really. In any case, just for like, three-and-a-half minutes, I think. How could you realize that?'

'Since I saw it.'

'What?'

'Passing.'

'Try not to talk like that Sam. You're alive at this point. Try not to talk like that.'

'Yet, I've seen it.'

'In any case, you're alive.'

'However, I saw. Where's my father Ronnie?'

'He's in concentrated. They keep him in a trance like state. I'm certain he'll make it.'

'How certain? I have a particularly screwed up outlook on this is on the grounds that not long before the accident he let me know he was gay and I simply need to know so you need to let me know precisely the way in which sure you will be, you comprehend Ronnie?'

'I'm super-certain.'

'Try not to say that!'

'What?'

'Super-certain.'

'Same difference either way.'

'Since it's dumb. Where's mother?'

'Try not to stress over her. You'll see her soon.'

'Where could she Ronnie be?'

'Just... you simply need to rest OK.'

'Let me know where she is or I'll shout.'

'She's in a facility.'

'What sort of facility?'

'You know... the nut-house. She had... how treated say? An injury prompted psychosis I accept. She continues to say that creep...'

'You call him a wet blanket once again and I never need to see you again, you hear me Ronnie?'

'That kid you were with... that... Vincent... in any case, she says he had something to do with it. That he made it happen. Also she says this load of odd stuff regarding vampires and I don't know Sam... I saw her in the facility and she was not doing so well. Yet, they discovered some medicine that truly appears

I was at your home simply a day after you had the mishap, and when I discovered through your mother, I was exceptionally vexed. In any case, I needed to leave. Call me AFTER you finish the book. We need to talk after you did that.

Under the note and a few papers, was the greatest, reddest book I had at any point seen. It was called Beelzebub's accounts to his grandson by a man called Gurdjieff. I looked under the book. There was a little box, dark, with a brilliant bow around it. Inside was a spic and span I-telephone X with fresh out of the plastic new I-telephone headphones. I looked under contacts and I observed Vincent's number. I needed to call him. In any case, he said to call me after I completed the book. In this way, I didn't. I checked out the music and there were all the Motörhead collections, Mozart's discography and the tune Everytime, by Britney. I put on Motörhead's Under Cover collection full volume and opened the book. The paper was exceptionally dainty, and the letters were tiny. It began this way: "Under every one of the feelings that have molded themselves in my 'complete presentiment' over my capable life is only one evident, specifically that all individuals - whatever the degree of improvement of their ability for comprehension might be for sure the types of appearance of the variables are who make their singular goals of a wide range of qualities become - feel generally and wherever on earth a squeezing inclination to say without holding back, or possibly in their musings, everytime when they are going to explore new territory, a for everyone reasonable calling to talk, of which the words have been different at different occasions, yet presently seems like; "In the name of the dad, the child and the heavenly phantom, amen.""'

'Goodness!' I told myself, 'That is pretty freaking troublesome stuff!' And I continued to peruse. I read each evening. I didn't see a lot of it, just that there was a demon on a spaceship that recounted stories to his grandson. Each sentence resembled that first sentence. A wide range of stuff happened to Beelzebub on the planet. He recounted a ton of stories to his grandson, that was continuously asking him inquiries. There were a wide range of room things going on as well. Enormous connections and legislative issues and god knows what. There were likewise a wide range of odd words that didn't appear to exist anyplace on the web.

Following seven days of perusing that book five hours per day, I wasn't even most of the way and a man moved close to me in the room; an elderly person who needed to watch the Discovery Channel. I told the attendant it was difficult for me to rest with the TV, that it gave me a cerebral pain. They needed to give the elderly person earphones however he accepted that the power in them would make his ear disease return and he said cellular breakdown in the lungs was terrible enough without help from anyone else. Thus, he just watched the screen without sound and I read the book. In some cases, he gave me irate and horny looks. He was terrible. His face was dangling from his skin like it could tumble off any moment.

'Are you prepared to attempt again with the TV Samantha?' he would ask in some cases and at times I said OK. Then, at that point, when he put it on, in five seconds I would say that I got a cerebral pain.

'What are you perusing there at any rate?' he said whenever I first advised him to switch the TV off.

'Something exceptionally old,' I said.

'How old?'

'It's from the twenties.'

'Also that doesn't give you a migraine?'

'No,' I said and I continued to peruse. I felt it when the elderly person was checking out me. He began breathing vigorously at whatever point a medical attendant was doing something to me. Ronnie continued to come however none of my different companions appeared and when I'd get some information about them, he generally said that they would sure come sooner rather than later. I didn't give a very remarkable fuck since I disdain my companions. He conversed with me about school. He brought me textbooks. He needed to assist me with reading up for school. I declined the proposition. I enlightened him concerning the book and he shook his head.

'That is not significant Sam. That is simply fantasies.'

'How treat have any familiarity with it?'

'It's dumb Sam. You need to stay aware of school.'

'I need to learn something Ron. I don't possess energy for school.'

He brought me chocolate some of the time, since I requested that. I could eat chocolate. Not to an extreme. Thus, he didn't bring me much. However, it was as yet pleasant. He was unable to help it. He couldn't resist the urge to be an absolute fucking douche. I contemplated Vincent, and how terrible I needed to call him, and I continued perusing, not understanding whatever was in that book and I trusted that he didn't anticipate that I should comprehend. The book was un-justifiable. However, i adored understanding it. It was something different, something else from anything I'd at any point peruse.

The second week I could move around in a wheelchair. There was a call from my mother when that occurred. She let me know a wide range of hysterical garbage. That they were harming her with the pills and getting father far from her. They concluded that it was best for me not to address her. My grandparents came visit me. They needed to fly as far as possible from Southern-California. I hadn't seen them in two years. I was happy they left when they did on the grounds that they were extremely exhausting individuals however I was additionally happy that they came. I began paying attention to Mozart. I began preferring Mozart. I could barely handle it. What's more at times, I paid attention to that Britney Spears tune out of incongruity since I made certain in those days that it was put there out of incongruity. Where could Vincent in Europe have been? Furthermore for what reason would I be able to just address him after I completed that book? For what reason could it matter? I got the book off the table immediately when my grandparents left.

'I know you, you bitch,' the man said, who's name I discovered was Timmy Blinder, 'You don't get no cerebral pains from that TV at all isn't that right? You just want to peruse that god damn book of yours presently don't ya? You think you is better that me cuz you read them books don't ya?'

'Is it safe to say that you are intending to pass on at any point in the near future you useless old fart?'

'Screw you, you fucking bitch! Imma watch this with sound on. I ain't going to kick the bucket paying attention to some idiotic bitch.'

Ronnie came in. 'Hello,' he said, and he gave me a Milka bar. 'I'm somewhat late yet I think I actually have like, a 30 minutes of visiting time.'

'Much obliged Ron,' I said, while the TV was shouting ads to us.

'Would you be able to turn that down sir?' Ronnie inquired.

'No,' Timmy said.

'I let him know it gives me migraines however he does it in any case. What's more he calls me a moronic bitch, which is additionally not making a difference.'

'Screw you bitch! You ain't getting no migraines or nothing! You just want to peruse that book of yours is all!'

'Try not to converse with her like that!'

'How you going to treat it kid?'

'I'm... I have a dark belt in Karate.'

'I have cellular breakdown in the lungs!'

'No doubt except for like... I'll beat you up when you're better!'

'I ain't improving kid. I'm getting dead!'

'Please accept my apologies.'

'Na you ain't. I'd beat you up on the off chance that I weren't so you better ain't sorry.'

'I have a dark belt in Karate.'

'I have a dark belt in fucking your mother!'

'I have a dark belt in fucking your father!'

'I bet you do you faggot!'

'Screw you, you fucking... screw poo!'

'You calling me screw crap kid?'

'Indeed! You're simply... screw poo.'

'God damn this fucking poop! I ain't taking this poo from a little fucking pixie kid! Imma kill you kid!' he said as he got the cylinder out of his arm and began to get up. 'You pixie kid! You going to kick the bucket!' The wires that were associated with his chest began to fly off.

'Sir, you truly shouldn't...' Ronnie said.

'Presently I'm sir all the abrupt eh?! I thought I was screw poop! I thought you said I was screw poo! Presently you going to pass on kid!' he got his feet on the ground. He got up and gradually, he began strolling towards Ronnie. Ronnie strolled in reverse until he remained against the divider.

'Remain back sir!'

The man impelled himself advances gradually. The look that was all over was beyond value. He seemed as though he was hopping in a WW1 channel with a blade. Also he punched Ronnie hard on the button. Ronnie didn't anticipate it. I heard the nose bone break. He was holding his nose with two hands and made an extremely boisterous "MMMM" sound. 'You going to bite the dust kid!' Timmy said and hit Ronnie over the head with a glass jar brimming with blossoms. I concluded that I needed to accomplish something. I got the coffin free from the ropes that were holding it up and put that leg on the ground. It hurt like poop. I ventured towards Timmy's bed, got the blood-pack that was appended to his arm before he pulled himself free from it and I tossed it at him. The pack burst on sway. There was blood all over. I figured it would stop him however he continued to hit Ronnie. Ronnie attempted to impede the punches yet they appeared to come from all over. I tossed more stuff. I tossed the remote. It hit the rear of Timmy's head. He pivoted. 'You fucking bitch! You going to kick the bucket as well!' and as he said that and began moving toward me, he slipped over the blood and wrecked on the floor. A medical attendant surged in.

'What for the sake of! What for the sake of GOD is happening in here!' she hollered.

'He went off the deep end! He attempted to kill us!' I said.

Ronnie was holding his ribs now. He took a gander at the medical caretaker. More individuals came into the room. They set me back on the bed and wheeled me out of the room. Then, at that point, they washed the blood off me and did a wide range of checks. They put me in another bed in another room that was all mine. Pleasant.

Two cops came into the room somewhat later. Cops in suits. One had a pen and a journal. He checked out his associate. 'Hey Samantha, I'm Steve and that is Dave. We're Colorado state police. A few genuinely horrendous things occurred back there, presently isn't that right? How's it hanging with you?'

'Murder police?'

'Excuse me?'

'Did he bite the dust? Is it true that you are exploring a crime?'

'Not yet. Be that as it may, we might be in a brief time. They say that Mr Blinder hasn't a lot of progress. We want to hear what you saw while the picture is still new in your h

'That is not a signature,' Dave said.

'Why not?' I inquired.

'Since everybody can draw that.'

'Alright,' I said and I jotted a wide range of things around the cross. For the most part roundabout lines. I loved it. It looked pretty. Following five seconds of doing that, I said; 'What about right now?'

'I surmise it'll need to do,' Steve said. 'Also incidentally, you are ready to peruse this assertion in court, right?'

'No. My leg is broken and I have some cerebrum harm. In half a month perhaps.'

'Great. Here is my truck. You call me when you know much else. At the point when some detail returns your memory, anything about Mr Blinder that you may recall. It could be in every way accommodating.'

'Okay,' I said. I like criminal investigators. I think criminal investigators are cool.

'It'll require half a month prior to this goes to court in any case.'

'How's Ronnie incidentally?'

'He's okay. He broke his nose and has a messed up rib. He says he needs to squeeze charges.'

'Squeezing charges against a terminal cellular breakdown in the lungs patient appears to be somewhat moronic,' I said.

'Perhaps so,' Dave said.

'What sort of combative techniques preparing did he have in any case?'

'He says he's a dark belt in Karate.'

'I thought you must be eighteen for that.'

'It's what he says.'

'Things being what they are, he has a dark belt in Karate and he gets his butt kicked by a terminal cellular breakdown in the lungs patient?'

'I surmise he did.'

'Indeed, you'll hear from us in a matter of seconds. We thank you for your consistence Samantha. Also in the event that you want assistance with what you of some kind saw...'

'Not this time. Yet, in the event that you could advise the medical attendant to present to me my book and my telephone, I'd see the value in it. It's large and it's red and it's by Gurdjieff.'

'How would you spell that?' Dave inquired.

'Who cares?' I said.

'Okay. I'll tell her. Bye Samantha.'

'Bye,' I said and afterward Steve said bye and afterward I was left alone once more.

I didn't pondered anything and how nothing was likewise something. Then, at that point, a medical attendant came in with my book under her arm and my telephone. I counted the pages that were left. I counted thirty. I needed to peruse the last page first. I observed an envelope taped to back of the cover there. 'Hi bibliophile,' the envelope said. I opened it. In the envelope was a manually written letter from Vincent. The penmanship was tiny. This is what it said:

Hello there Sammiewhamycocojammy,

Cool book huh? Doesn't has anything to do with me at all yet I said that you would observe something in the book about my sort and this letter is in the book, correct? Thus, I didn't lie.

I think you assume I'm a vampire now, and this isn't true. We are a line of Kings from an earlier time. Early bronze age speculative chemistry had prevailed with regards to tracking down a technique to become gold into iron, then, at that point, iron into gold and a method for broadening the life expectancy and the strength by seven.

In any case, you need to drink human blood. A liter daily or somewhere in the vicinity, for a person of your weight. Whenever you're turned, you'd have toxin in your blood you see. Also the toxin gets in your DNA. It comes initially from the Beelzebat, an extremely odd variety of bat that main exist in imprisonment. It was hostage 100% of the time.

The animal was raised from damnation it was told. I don't have the foggiest idea. Furthermore this hereditary modification makes re-tractive teeth fill in your mouth to spread the toxin.

Presently you want to get turned, isn't that right? If by some stroke of good luck it were just basic. The Bronze Kings are shrewd. We realize that if everyone could know how to transform metal into gold, that it would be futile, similarly as, assuming there are an excessive number of "vampires" comparable to "humans", they would starve. There are just 72 Bronze Kings on the planet and when one passes on, with each and every other demise, (you may likewise have a kid that conveys the toxin, which you just get with another transporter) the direction gives a permit to turn.

Presently somebody just kicked the bucket a decade prior and there is place for a turn, yet it's not my chance to turn, and you'll be dead when it is on the off chance that you don't turn quick. I'm forty, 41 this March, and the person who's turn it is currently is Kharkanov Karnakle. He's 534 years of age. He hasn't settled on a choice yet. They say he's too old to even consider understanding the cutting edge world as he's additionally too old to even think about getting what might make the best present day Bronze King. This happens a ton and they for the most part allowed their mate to pick for them. Thus, he lets his child, Ghargatron, who is just 187 choose. He is insane, and there were a great deal of Kings that brought bloodcows to him that they were enamored with or they just preferred to see as Kings (one person brought Michael Jackson) yet Ghargatron declined each and every one. He actually has three years before his father's turn will pass. We could attempt.

In any case, there were a few movements in an examination that could demonstrate exceptionally favorable to my sort and I expected to do a few business that takes outrageous concentration. I was unable to make them consider me when I did that (I figure the troublesome aspect will be throughout when you read this) since it would be too diverting. I realize you feel like poop since you're in the clinic and your mother's presumably in the crazy house at this point however you need to comprehend the significance of my work.

Furthermore you should likewise be considering how I treat an understudy in your school, correct? All things considered, I saw Twilight and I just thought about the way in which that would work out, in actuality. My cousin needed to see it. I saw it with her and I just told myself: 'For what reason don't I show that nitwit how getting blood-cow chicks at a blood-cow school is done while I live near a little town in the wild in any case,' and I did. Sorry for the blood-cow thing incidentally, it's exactly what we call you.

Much love from Vincent and I trust that you will recuperate rapidly. Trust your father makes it as well. We will forever make it together. Also in the event that we can't make it, we take it and in the event that we can't take it, we break it.

P.S.

You ever had a cinnamon-bun? I'm having my first cinnamon-bun here at Denver airport and it's fucking delicious. Bye now.

'Motherfucker,' I said. I folded the letter and put it back in the envelope. A nurse came in to see me.

'Are you alright Sam? What you just been through... Are you alright?'

'Alright,' I said.

'Are you alright?'

'Alright... alright... alright...'

And the nurse asked me again. And I said, 'I'm alright,' and then she said 'OK,' and I told her I wanted to be alone for a while. She left me alone. I closed my eyes and I thought: 'Fuck me. Why does he have to be forty?'

4, Demons

I called Vincent 'Is that Sammiewhamycocojammy?' he asked.

'Yes,' I said, 'Is that Vinciepinciedimsiewhimsy?'

'Yes. How's the happenings?'

'The happenings? I'm in a fucking hospital Vince, how do you think the happenings are?'

'There's all sorts of happenings in the hospital. All sorts of hospital happenings. I was hoping you would tell me about them.'

'A lung-cancer patient attacked my friend Ronnie and I threw blood at them.'

'That is fucking hot.'

'What?'

'I said that's pretty fucking hot. Please continue.'

'It's not hot, its fucking disgusting. You're fucking disgusting!'

'What do you expect? You know. I mean, I know you know. So, what do you expect?'

'Like, I don't know, that you don't have to drink blood AND have a fetish for it.'

'That's what we do. Everybody knows that. But it's all very humane.'

'What's humane about killing people for blood?'

'We don't kill people! We just breed really stupid ones and farm them.'

'You farm humans?'

'Yes, but really stupid ones. Like, they have an average IQ of seventy-two. That kind of person. They're easy to entertain. We just drain a little blood from them every day and that has worked for centuries. The stupider they are the happier they seem to become. I mean, you have to understand that...'

'I think I understand Vince. I'm nothing but a stupid blood-cow-girl to you that you want because you want to brag about being a better twilight vampire than the twilight vampire in *Twilight*!'

'That's not true Sam, that was just the intent. That's not what we have. I want to turn you. I want to bring you to Ghargatron. You can be a queen in the Kings counsel! I have faith in you.'

'I have to think about it Vince.'

'Haven't you had enough time to think?'

'No, I was a little bit busy with reading your stupid book!'

'What's stupid about it?'

'You are,' I said and hung up the phone.

I hated myself and everyone around me. I wanted to go to an island. I closed my eyes and pretended to be on an island. I heard a coconut fall in the distance. Monkeys and shit. All the island stuff was there. Then I opened my eyes again and I saw my mother walk into the room. She looked pretty doped up.

'Hiiiii Sam,' she said.

'Hiiiii mom,' I said.

'I have to tell you something Sam.'

'What is it mom?'

'I have schizophrenia.'

'That's great mom.'

'What?'

'I said it's awful.'

'It is. What are you doing in a hospital sweetie?'

'I'm getting dead!'

'WHAT?!'

'I'M GETTING DEAD!'

'WHAT?!'

'DEAD!'

'YOU ARE DEAD?! ARE YOU DEAD? SHE'S DEAD!' my mom screamed and a nurse came in. She took my mom away. She kept on screaming in the hall. Another nurse came in and asked me what happened.

'I scared her. Her reaction scared me, and my reaction to that reaction made the conflict intensify like a laser beaming in between mirrors. That is what happened.'

'I'm sorry I don't understand.'

'That´s the best I can explain it.'

´Alright then,´ she said and just left in confusion. I slept a while.

I woke up from the pinging of my phone. It was a text from Vincent: 'Hope you're not still mad at me. Hope you've decided you want to live for a long time with me. Trust me, there is no greater honor in this world than to get turned. Ghargatron wants to use his telekinetic-brainwave-interconnecting-device so the three of us can dream together and he can see whether you're worthy. Whisper the next numbers twelve times with your eyes closed at exactly ten in the evening so the device can pick your brainwave-frequency out of the morphic-resonance: 5-7-2-4-3.'

I waited until ten, whispered it twelve times and opened my eyes. There I was, with two working legs, in a blue summer dress. I was in a desert.

A cloud of smoke came closer fast, and as it slowed down, I saw it was Vincent's Lexus. He did a couple of donuts around me, stopped in front of me and opened the door. 'Get in babe. Dream on.'

I got in the car. 'Look, Sam. You have to trust me when I say that you are the best thing that ever happened to me in all my forty years on this planet. But you also have to understand what it is that I am in relation to you. My point is this: you can't go up to Ghargatron; the self-proclaimed and unchallenged King of Kings and call him a vampire, or disobey him in any way because you will lose your head. He'll have you decapitated before you can even wake up.'

'What?!'

'Don't worry about it. Just be on your best behavior around Ghargatron and you'll find that he's a really nice person. Just don't say anything bad about human farming or stuff like that. He'll kill you before you had the chance to wake up and there'll be nothing I can or want to do about it. You just bow down and after he is done introducing himself you say: "We are honored to be in your shadow great" and then you say the thing that he introduces himself as. And you never know what that is going to be but it's always very long so remember the words carefully Sam because we have to say them together OK?'

'I don't know about this Vince.'

'You'll know when you're dead,' Vincent said and he hit the gas. I saw a huge golden helicopter appear on the horizon.

'So, it's "We are honored to be in your shadow great" and then whatever the fuck he introduces himself as?'

'Yes. And under no circumstances use the word vampire.'

'OK Vince,' I said and Vince turned on *Horse with no name* without touching the radio.

'Is it that he has no name or that the horse has no name?' I asked.

'Good question, I never thought about it but it could work both ways. I've been to the desert on a horse with no name... yeah... OK... here we are,' he said and he got out of the car.

In the open side door of this golden helicopter stood a very black, very tall, very muscular man, with a golden crown on his head. There was a round hole in the middle of the crown and I saw a white tattoo of a bullseye through that hole. There were dollar signs on each side of it. He was wearing army print shorts, no shirt and a golden revolver; a Magnum Python with a white handle. Next to the side door stood two women in golden bikinis. The right one was Oriental and the left one was also black. They carried golden AK47's. In front of them were two dogs, very big and fearsome. They were not on a chain.

'BOW DOWN FOR GHARGATRON, THE KING OF KINGS!' the Asian woman yelled as we came in a range of ten feet from Ghargatron. We bowed down.

'LOOK AT ME!' said Ghargatron. We looked. He grinned and spread his arms. 'I am Ghargatron, the doom machine, the father of the apocalypse, the master of death, the dealer of evil, the King of Kings!'

'We are honored to be in your shadow great Ghargatron, the doom machine, the father of the apocalypse, the master of death, the dealer of evil, the King of Kings!' Vincent and I said together.

'Look at my women! How do you like my women Vincent?'

'They're great Ghargatron.'

'Now look at my dogs! How do you like my dogs?'

'Also, very great.'

'Might it be your opinion that I, Ghargatron, King of Kings, have the greatest women and the greatest dogs?'

'I think you are very right about that Ghargatron.'

'Good,' he said and he jumped out of the helicopter. He lit a blunt with a storm lighter and walked towards us, 'Who's the blood-cow Vince?'

'She is that Sam I told about and she's something else.'

'How so?'

'Look in her eyes, you'll see.'

'Get up Sam.'

I got up. He held my chin in his enormous hand and looked in my eyes. Then he pushed me backwards, not hard, but hard enough that I had to take a few steps back.

'She has a demon Vincent.'

'I know. It's why I like her.'

'She has a beautiful demon. She became a demon to beat it. I see what she is. *She is the demon.'*

'She is.'

'And you want me to waste my father's turn on her?'

'It would not be a waste Ghargatron. It wouldn't be a waste at all.'

'We'll see about that.'

'The greatest dogs perhaps, but I have a monster on a leash. And the training of the beast is almost complete.'

'I've heard rumors. I hear lots of rumors. I heard you did a brain removal and kept the brain alive. I heard a lot of things. I heard you saw my mother.'

'I did.'

'She is good, I know.'

'She is.'

'So, what about the beast?'

'I'll show you in a week. I have to bring it over from Europe. Takes a while.'

'And you'll be done with the training?'

'Yes.'

'And what are you planning to do with this glorious beast?'

'A gift to you.'

'And you want me to bring her to my father, so he can turn her?'

'Regardless, I give you the beast. As a token of my respect. That's all.'

'Good. Now leave me with the demon girl and I'll see whether she's worthy. Bring her the paper Kelly!'

The black woman walked towards me. She got a piece of paper and a pen out of her golden bikini bottom and gave it to me, 'Sign it if you want to know where the demon got in,' Ghargatron said.

'I HEREBY GIVE GHARGATRON, KING OF KINGS, FULL CONTROL OVER THE TELEKINETIC LUCID DREAMSEQUENCE I AM IN RIGHT NOW,' the paper said. I looked at Vincent.

'Nothing can happen,' he said, 'You're only dreaming. You could have a bad nightmare though. It's up to him.'

'OK,' I said. I sighed the paper with the cross and circles.

'That's a really pretty autograph,' Ghargatron said as he looked at it.

I saw that Vincent had a worried look on his face, 'Now get in the chopper you little demongirl,' Ghargatron said. I got in. Ghargatron got behind the steering knob and flew the helicopter straight up. I saw Vincent wave at me while I lifted into the sky. He became a small dot and then he disappeared.

'Look at that,' Ghargatron said, 'Pretty high.'

'Yes, very.'

'Why don't you jump out?'

'What?!'

'You heard me. Jump out.'

I looked out of the window. It is only a dream, I thought. Nothing can go wrong. I opened the door and looked at a dazzling altitude. I felt a push and I fell down. I kept on falling down. The ground got closer. I felt the wind in my face. My heart was beating fast. I screamed. I saw the ground approach me faster and faster. And the moment I hit it, I was somewhere else; naked, and chained to a wall in some dungeon. I could see only out of my left eye. I saw a rat shoot over the floor. It stopped, looked at me, and crawled into a hole in the wall. There was a little window high above, that shun some light. I saw the hall light up. Ghargatron, carrying a torch came into the room.

'I saw your soul Sam. I'll show you where your demon got in. This is 1234, and you were about the age you are now when you died there and went to the time you find yourself in now. This was you, look at you,' he said and he held a mirror up. I saw there was a leather patch sowed over my left eye.

'You got that when you were twelve. They cut your eye out because they thought it was evil, that it was destroying the harvest. You're a witch Sam, and your name is Mathilda. You will see how she died, your former form, and then you will understand your hate and disgust with those around you. You'll see where the demon got in. I would say have fun but this is not going to be fun.'

'I'm not sure if I want to do this,' I said.

'Like that matters. You signed remember? You should have thought about that before you signed. It wasn't like you had to,' Ghargatron said and then he left the room.

My mom walked into the dungeon with a guard, 'Mathilda,' she said, 'I pity thee.'

I wanted to say something but no words came out, until they did, but they were not mine, yet, in a strange way, they also felt like they were, 'I have no use for your pity. It has never helped me mother,' I said.

'Listen to thine mother Mathilda. They will do it once more. They will try once more. They could succeed. Maybe they don't have to burn you at the stake at dawn tomorrow. They said there is a change they could still get the devil out.'

'I am not worthy of redemption mother. I gave the evil eye.
If only the flames can purify my soul, then give me flames
in all their glory!'

'Mathilda, that is the devil speaking. The devil will be
banished from your soul Mathilda, the priest is coming.
He's coming!' she said. The guard tapped on the ground
with his battle ax and my mother followed him out of the
dungeon. Again, there was the light of fire in the hall, and a
priest came in with the guard and a torch. He put the torch
in one of the holders in the wall. He approached slowly. I
felt his cold hand over my naked body. He pinched a nipple,
quite hard. I did not scream.

'To cast a demon out requires the insertion of the saint,' he
said and he grabbed me by the pussy, 'Let the holy spirit
penetrate your... soul.'

He kissed my forehead. He walked to the guard, that was
standing in the corner of the room and said, 'Remove the
shackles, and I must do my exorcism in private. The demon
is not fit for the untrained eye to see.'

The guard opened the shackles with big black keys. I fell to
my knees right away, because I was hanging on the wall so
long that my limbs were like rubber. I looked to the floor as
I heard the footsteps of the guard echo their way out of the
dungeon. 'Turn that behind of thine in my direction you
filthy witch!' the priest said. I did not comply. I could not
move. My limbs still seemed to be made out of rubber. I felt
a blow to my head. I fell down. I saw that rat, shoot by fast,
and I felt that I was being turned on my belly and my legs
were being moved apart. I looked up and whispered into
the darkness of the room; 'God help me,' and then I felt his
spit on my cunt, and he moved inside. I felt his violence, his

hate, his anger and his disgust go in. I was not even human to him. Not even human. It did not take him long to finish. When he did, I heard his footsteps echo to the corner of the room, and then I heard them come back. First there was this sound, that horrible sound of a whip, and I turned around and looked at him standing there with the whip, as if he was God himself. He slashed it over my tit, making it bleed. Now I screamed, and my screams echoed through the walls of this dungeon, that I found myself in.

'On your knees, you dog of Satan!' the priest yelled. I tried to get up but still my limbs were not adjusted to not hanging on the wall yet. The shackles had made their marks. Red and swollen were the places they used to chain. The whip came back and struck my face.

'I will tolerate no whore of Lucifer in my land!' he said, 'Have fun with the monks tonight for early in the morning *thou shall burn witch!* And the faggots you will burn on shall be regarded higher in the eyes of God than a filthy little creature like you!' and then he left the dungeon.

The monks came in and tight me to a wheel, with knees and elbows. Doggy position. The wheel was spinning horizontally over the stone in the dungeon. I became very dizzy. 'STOP THE WHEEL OF SODOM!' I heard a dark voice scream in the light of the torches. They stopped the wheel. I had to vomit. I threw up.

'THERE GO'S THE DEVIL!' they sang, 'WE ARE THE MONKS OF THE CLOCK OF SODOM! WE NUMBER THE CLOCK OF SODOM!'

'Thine number ist number thirteen Mark, for thou art the new, and you must rise to the holy numbers. Get on the wheel and keep the whore between your legs, then ride her, and poop on her as you see fit, get thine bible out and read *Revelations*. With the start of every chant you will come off and turn the wheel. You must count the turns. Once the whore has gone around the clock of Sodom, you count one. It takes 77 rounds for her soul to purify enough so that the flames may do their work when we are done,' a monk said.

'I understand brother,' I heard another monk say. The monk that said that I couldn't see because he was behind me. I felt his bare ass sitting down on my back and a few seconds later, I felt warm shit streaming down my body. He grabbed me by the hair and held my head back. He licked my cheeks. Both of them.

'God has given us a tasty whore to purify brothers!' he said and then they all started chanting again: 'In the clock of Sodom we purify the witch, in the clock of Sodom, the clock of Sodom, in the clock of Sodom, we purify the witch!' they kept on singing that while the monk that was sitting on top of me screamed things from the Bible: 'And I took the little book out of the angel's hand, and ate it up; and it was in my mouth sweet as honey: and as soon as I had eaten it, my belly was bitter!' He kept on reading loudly as the circle of the monks grew tighter, and I saw that they all simultaneously stopped chanting and toke their robes off in one motion. They were all butt naked now. And they were all hard.

I counted, to stay sane. But after 77 rounds, when I expected number 13 to get off, it still kept going. I realized soon that it worked thus that if a monk was about to come in my asshole or my mouth, he would start chanting, and then the monk that was riding me like a horse and shitting over me got off and he would slap me in the face, my tits and my ass, and stick his finger in there and one in my mouth and that's how he turned the wheel of Sodom towards the next monks in the circle. I saw that monk thirteen had no face. It was at turn 138 that the light started shining through the window again, and the monk who rode me stopped reading out of the bible. '77!' he yelled. 'We have purified her soul!'

'Let's feed her and take her to the stake.'

They untied me from the wheel. 'Lay her down gently brothers,' I heard. I was laid down on the stone, 'Open her mouth so we can feed her.'

Exactly what the reader must expect to happen happened. All of it. They forced me to swallow all of it. I was dressed in rags and a cone-shaped hat was placed on my head. The ropes burned in my arms. I was bare footed. Two monks carried me up the stairs, because I could not walk it. They put me on my feet when I was dragged into the church. I could barely walk. The monks were holding me up. I heard screams and looked up. The church was full of people, 'SPARE THAT WITCH NO FAGGOTS, BURN, BURN, BURN!' they were all screaming. I was moved out through the hall in between the benches. I fell. They dragged me. 'Walk Mathilda,' the monk without the face was saying, 'I know you can do it. Just a little further...'

I tried my best to do it. I did it. I stood there on my feet. I walked, step by step, out of the church. The people that were in the church followed us. They screamed the same thing over and over: 'SPARE THAT WITCH NO FAGGOTS, BURN, BURN, BURN!' They were walking around us. I spotted my mother. She was also chanting but she was looking away from me. I looked at her. I kept on looking at her. I screamed 'MOTHER!' but she didn't look back.

'Don't do that Mathilda. If you do that again we have to hurt you.'

It was blurry because of all the tears. I saw the stake appear in the middle of a square. There were lots of people on that square. They all started screaming. I was unable to walk any further. Complete terror had paralyzed me. Two of the monks picked me up and carried me up the stake. They tight me to the pole in the middle of the bundles of wood.

Suddenly, the crowd was silent. You could hear a pin drop. A monk came closer. It was the monk without the face again. 'You're going to burn in hell forever for what you did,' he said and I recognized that voice somewhere. Then he walked away. I heard the wood ignite. I saw the smoke. I started screaming. Nobody was doing anything. Nobody was saying anything. The smoke got thicker and I saw the flames. Nobody was doing anything. Nobody was saying anything. I kept screaming, as the flames moved towards me, and when they licked my legs, and I could breathe nothing but smoke, I had an orgasm so intense that I am unable to put it into words. It was the greatest thing I've ever felt multiplied by a thousand. I kept screaming. I just kept screaming. I woke up in my hospital bed. It was drenched in sweat and pussy-juice.

5, Extra Virgin

I was wheeled out of the hospital finally, by my uncle Buck Pope. He was a freelance writer for commercials from San Francisco. He heard about the accident and called me. I had never seen him before but he sounded nice on the phone. The plan was to send me to my grandparents in California after I was released but he suggested that he would just come to Dead Rat and live there with me until my mother was cured from her schizophrenia or my dad would recover. I accepted the offer, both because I didn't want to live with my grandparents and because I wanted to stay close to what was happening. I also wondered why my friends had not visited me. Maybe because of Annabel. She had a large amount of social power over the rest of the idiot girls.

He wheeled me to his Subaru and helped me in the back seat, where that leg would fit sideways. He had just said: 'Hello Sam, I'm Buck, I'm here to pick you up,' I said 'Good,' and those were all the words we exchanged in person. He was really businesslike about the proposition too on the phone. A man of few words. I liked that.

After the first hour of a two-hour ride, in which we said nothing, without it seeming strange, he was smoking cigarettes constantly behind the wheel, blowing the smoke out of the window.

'Can I have a cigarette?' I finally asked. I forgot not to care. My mom always held my allowance for two weeks if she caught me smoke because "She's not giving me money so I can buy lung-cancer" But she wasn't here now.

'Sure,' he said and he gave me one.

'Did you drive all the way from Fresno?'

'Yeah. I like to have my own car.'

'I heard you were a writer.'

'I write commercials. You know, "You want your slippers to grip because you don't want your grip to slip", that sort of stuff.'

'That's awesome! Do you have more?'

'Say yes and impress: dress for success.'

'YEY! How many did you write?'

'A zillion.'

'Do you have another one?'

'My best is...' he said and suddenly there was a loud honking behind us. I looked in the mirror and I saw Vincent's Lexus flashing its alarm lights. He stuck his arm out of the window and motioned us to stop.

'What does this idiot want?' Buck asked.

'I know that idiot. Can you pull over mister Pope?'

'Alright,' he said and he pulled over behind a lonely unmanned gas-station. Nobody knows exactly where nowhere is but sometimes you do find yourself in the middle of it.

He stopped before us and he got out. He walked around the car and opened the passenger door. An immense black, short haired dog got out of the car. It was the biggest dog I had ever seen in my life. He looked very calm though. He kind of looked like an over-sized Rottweiler with an over-sized German Shepperd in it, and the fur of a Siamese cat. He looked like he could bite through metal if he had to.

Vincent and the dog walked up to the driver's window. He stuck his hand through there.

'Hi, I'm Vincent. I was just at the hospital. I was going to visit because I just came back from Romania with my new dog but I heard they just released her. I saw the wheelchair and Sam's red hair in the rear window and I figured I'd say hi.'

'VINCE!' I yelled, 'What were you doing in Europe all this time?'

'I told you, business. Up,' he said and I saw that huge dog head appear in the window. It scared the shit out of me but Buck did not seem impressed at all. 'You see, that's Doggio; my dog. I'll tell you all about him later. He's the greatest dog in the world. And you are mister?'

'Well, hello Vincent, I'm Buck Pope, Samantha's uncle. I'm going to look after her for a little while. So, you've been in Romania? Don't you have to go to school or something? You look barely old enough to drive.'

'I did some school in Romania. You can do some school everywhere.'

'Uhm... alright then. Do you want to have dinner with us?'

'That sounds wonderful. I'll just drive behind you.'

'You do that Vincent. We'll be there in an hour.'

'Righto,' he said and he walked back to his car. He was wearing an open white blouse with rolled up sleeves over a white undershirt, black pants and very thick black sunglasses. Doggio jumped into the car as soon as Vincent opened the passenger door. And as he drove behind us, I could see him in the mirror, tapping his fingers on the steering wheel and smoking joints. He smoked a hell of a lot of them behind that wheel. I even saw him roll one while there was still one burning in his mouth once or twice. And that dog was just staring at the road. He never looked anywhere except dead ahead.

After an hour of looking at him smoke weed in the mirror, he pulled up behind us in front of my house. He and Buck helped me into the wheelchair.

'Can my dog come in?' Vincent asked.

'Fine by me,' Buck said, 'You're not allergic are you Sam?'

'No.'

They dragged the wheelchair backwards over the steps in front of the door and wheeled me inside. I smelled that the house had been empty for a while. There was a bed placed for me in the living room. I hated that. I like my privacy.

'I'm going to get something to eat. What do you want to eat Sam?'

'Pizza,' I said.

'I can make some, with real dough. You want me to show you kids how to do that?'

'That´ll be nice Mister Pope,' I said.

'Call me Buck,' he said and he also said; 'You kids behave now. I'll be back in less than half-an-hour so if you want to have an alcoholic welcome home party you have to be quick about it.'

'Yes, mister Pope,' Vincent said.

'You can call me Buck too kid,' Buck said and he closed the door behind him. And right after he did that, Vincent pulled a 42 out of an ankle holster and pressed the barrel hard against my forehead.

'If you're werewolf you better tell me now Sam...'

'What the fuck?! What the fuck Vince?! What the fuck are you talking about?!'

'You tell me right now or I'll fucking blow your fucking brains out Sam! You tell me right the fuck now if you're a fucking werewolf Sam... you better tell me right the fuck now...' he said. His voice was shaking and his eyes were wide. I saw tears appear in them.

'You're not going to pull that trigger.'

'I'll pull that trigger Sam. You better fucking believe that I will pull this fucking trigger if you don't tell me *right now* what you are and what you did to Ghargatron in the Pacific... I swear to God...'

'You're a pussy Vince. You'll never pull the trigger because you're a pussy. You could prove me wrong but I'll never know so you'll never have the satisfaction of seeing me admit that.'

He thought for a second after I said that, not more than a second, then he took a step back and held the barrel against his temple. 'Tell me now or I'll prove to you that you're wrong and you'll never have the satisfaction of admitting that to me.'

'Jesus Vince. I'm not a fucking werewolf.'

'Look me in the eye,' he said as he put the gun back in its holster and stepped towards me. I looked him in the eyes.

'Say it. Say "I am not a werewolf."'

'I am not a werewolf.'

'OK... OK... I'm sorry, I thought... it's just... it's been rough baby. But I believe you.'

'You can't just point guns at people!'

'I know,' he said as he sat down on my dad's chair, 'I just... It's been rough baby...', and he put his head in his hands. Doggio walked slowly toward him and he put his head on

Vincent's knee. Vincent stroked him on the head. Doggio made a very soft and light noise.

'What happened?'

Vincent got his phone out of his pocket and put it on the coffee-table. With extreme ease and quickness, he tapped it a few times and a recording started playing:

'This is Vincent Offenbach reporting the murder of our King Ghargatron Karnakle. It was the work of a werewolf. I was on Ghargatron's oil-tanker, teaching him how to work with the Rottweiler-Beelzebat-Wolfdog I had given him. I was shooting flying potato's out of the air when I heard loud noises and screams from the belly of the ship. It was like hell had broken loose. I reloaded the MG I was shooting with quickly and hurried with it below deck. When I got down the stairs, I saw Ghargatron fly through the hallway with a sword in his hand and crash into the wall behind. 'WE HAVE A WEREWOLF ON BOARD!' he screamed as he was running back to where he flown from. I ran next to him in the hall and dropped the MG, for I knew it would be of no use in the battle. I grabbed one of the silver swords that hung on the wall. After a minute of running we were at the stern, to which the hall was leading. There was a room there and I saw the wood of the door that Ghargatron must have flown through still lying around. It was Ghargatron's study room. It was turned to shreds. All the furniture was completely destroyed and the metal walls were dented everywhere. 'We're gonna get this motherfucker Vincent!' Ghargatron said.

'We better!' I said.

It goes without saying that we stuck together. We went up to the deck and what we found there was gruesome beyond believe. The deck was red with blood and covered with the bodies of women and dogs. I told Ghargatron that it was better to wait for the werewolf's return here in the open because I did not feel like fighting one of those fuckers in close quarters. Ghargatron was nothing but raging fury after he saw what the wolf had done to his dogs and women. He screamed, 'COME OUT KITTY, KITTY, KITTY! WE WANT TO PLAY! COME OUT KITTY!' and he had a maniacal look on his face. We walked together over the deck. I saw it move over the bridge fast, tapped Ghargatron on the shoulder and pointed. He nodded. We ran towards the bridge and the thing jumped down on us. We could both dodge the attack and the wolf crashed through the floor. We looked in the hole it had made and we jumped after it. The hole went on for three floors. It was dark where he landed. The creature managed to sneak up on us from behind and bit Ghargatron's shoulder. I saw a twinkle in the eye of the wolf, I aimed and I hit that twinkle with the sword. The wolf panicked and jumped out of the hole. Ghargatron and I went after it. We were just on the deck when we heard it jump in the water. We ran to the helicopter so we could chase it. Ghargatron had a golden mini-gun in his golden helicopter that I shot at the wolf. It slowed him down some but we couldn't stop it. We did reach it and got very close to the wolf.

'TAKE THE STEERING!' Ghargatron screamed. I sat down in the co-pilot's chair and told Ghargatron I was ready. He got out of the cockpit and stood in the door with his sword in his hand.

'HOLD HER LOW AND STEADY VINCENT!' he screamed at me and I did my very best. At one-hundred-and-fifty miles an hour, he jumped out of the helicopter on the werewolf's back. I heard it growl and cry but I could not see what was going on do to all the water splashing up. Then Ghargatron flew up to the helicopter and was cut in a thousand pieces by the blades of his chopper. I followed the wolf as far as the tank of the helicopter could take me. I last saw it on the Mexican coast. I am now in a bar in San-Martinez, Mexico and I need extraction fast. The helicopter is camouflaged with leaves and some local boys are guarding it.

Please also extract the Rottweiler-Beelzebat-Wolfdog off the oil tanker. You'll find it in the control room. Might also be life regular dogs and women there. I didn't have time to check but I've seen none. Over.'

'Jesus Vince...' I said and then there was silence. A lot of it. I wanted to say something but only that soft, high sound was heard, that Doggio was making. I thought of something to say finally:

'You know what I don't understand about the Matrix? It's that, if Cyrus knows the steak he is eating might as well be dog shit, why are they sitting in a restaurant? Smith doesn't care either because he's a computer program. So why are they not in the gutter, eating dog shit, or just a white room, with black curtains, at the station... you know... It doesn't make any sense to me.'

'That's a great question and Cream reference. It shakes the foundation of the philosophical construct presented in that movie hard enough for the building to collapse!'

'I know right! Or take this paradox: if Morpheus shows you "the world for what it is in actuality" (and I actually did finger quotes with that), how could you tell then, that

Morpheus himself is not part of the Matrix and him showing you that is just part of the program?'

'You just thought about that?!'

'I spend a lot of time in a hospital bed. I did a lot of thinking in between reading that fucking book.'

'But you are glad you read it though?'

'Yeah… I really am. It made me grow.'

'You make me grow.'

'You also make me grow. But you make me grow into a monster.'

'You were already a monster before I met you,' he said. He came closer and crouching before me, he put his hand on my cheek and said: 'A very beautiful monster.'

'I know,' I said, 'You're a beautiful monster too,' and just when we were about to kiss, Buck came in with the ingredients for our home-made pizza to be.

'Alright, you wanna help me make this pizza? I am starving. Let's put some music on and make this thing happen. What kind of music do you kids like.'

'Classical,' Vincent said.

'Heavy-metal,' I said, simultaneously with Vincent.

'Then I know just the thing. Do you know where heavy-metal comes from Sam?'

'Burroughs,' Vincent said.

'The term, yes, but what about the sound?'

'Link Wray,' I said.

'The texture of the sound, yes, but what about the tonal intervals and the rhythmic structure?'

'I don't know Buck, tell me,' I said.

'Paganini.'

'Who?'

'I think he's right Sam,' Vincent said.

'And he's also Italian so great pizza making music per definition.'

'Per definition,' I repeated.

'Also, if you want to make pizza, you have to drink good Italian wine while cooking it, eating it and digesting it. And guess what I just found in my bag?' he said as he pulled out a bottle of Don Peignoir from the shopping bag.

Buck pored the wine and we sat at the living room table because I couldn't stand up at the kitchen counter. It was really good. Paganini was good too.

'The most important thing about making real Italian pizza is choosing the right olive oil. Of course, you need extra virgin, but real extra virgin. This tiny little supermarket here doesn't have extra virgin, it just has this stuff unfortunately. I'll order a real extra virgin online later. It's very important that it is extra virgin.'

'But it says extra virgin on the bottle!' I said.

'It always does,' Vincent said.

'It also says made in Italy. I know this probably comes from New Mexico. I wonder when New Mexico became New Italy sometimes,' Buck said.

'Maybe we should tell them,' I said.

'Maybe we should,' Vincent said.

'Alright, anyways… I'll just tell you what to do and you can make the dough OK? That way you learn it best.'

'OK Buck,' I said and what followed was a very long sequence of cooking instructions that I paid very good attention to because I was starving. We had to put the yeast in the water and stir, we had to make a volcano with the flour and poor that yeast-water into the crater, then we kneaded, which took forever because it was never good enough, we greased up a bowl with the fake extra-virgin olive-oil and turned the dough around in it, then Buck put a cover on the bowl and said: 'Just let it rest for four hours.'

'Four hours!' I yelled, 'I thought you said you were starving!'

'Yes, and in four hours I'll really be starving. Now that is when pizza tastes the best.'

'But it's already eight in the evening!'

'What's wrong with eating at midnight?'

'Nothing, I guess. But I really need to eat something *now*.'

'OK, how about a mango? I bought some mangos for breakfast.'

'Is that all you bought? Pizza stuff, wine and mangos?'

'I also bought cigarettes.'

'Great. Can I have the mango please?'

'Alright,' he said and he walked into the kitchen. A little later he came back with a plate, on which a mango tower was build, with little strips of it, that were laid over each other crosswise with a dipping bowl of red sauce. Next to it he placed a bowl of water so I could wash my hands and avoid dough on the mango because "You don't want no dough on your mango you know". I realized that Buck was a pretty strange guy.

'I'm going to set up shop in your parent's room and get to work. Your mom wouldn't mind if I smoke there right? Last time I saw her she was smoking one after the other.'

'No, she doesn't. We always smoke in the house.'

'Good,' Buck said, 'It is strange though, that you don't have any ash-trains around then.'

'Dad likes to make them out of empty beer-cans. Whoever was here to clean out the fridge and put that bed here must have thought they were trash.'

'That explains.'

'You need any help carrying your stuff upstairs?' Vincent asked.

'No, I don't have a lot of stuff. I just have to walk once. And please don't ever bother me while I write OK. Only excuse is when someone is dying or dead. I'll be done when the dough is. You kids will entertain yourself, right? And don't drive anywhere because you had wine and I don't want to be responsible for two teenagers dying in a car-crash. I think you should just call your parents and sleep over Vincent.'

'That might be best,' Vincent said while I was munching the mango tower down, which tasted great with that sauce. Vincent lit a cigarette and gave me one too after Buck walked out into the hall.

'I'm going to wash my hands,' Vincent said and he went to the kitchen. He sat on his knees behind me when he came back, he put his hands around my waist and his chin on my shoulder. 'Where were we?' he whispered in my ear and then he kissed my cheek. He placed a plate on the table and put the cigarette out on it. I did the same thing.

'Can you put me on the bed Vince? I'm tired.' He very gently lifted me off the chair and laid me down on the bed. 'Come here,' I said and he laid down beside me. It barely fitted. He looked at me and I looked at him and he smiled and I smiled and we kissed. He held me close and I held him close. He was so gentle. So tender. I felt his fingers go up and down my shoulder.

'Vincent?'

'What is it Sammie?'

'I have to tell you something.'

'OK. Tell me.'

'I'm a virgin. Kind of.'

'That's OK,' he said and he kissed me again.

'Do you want to...' I said and he put his finger to my lips, 'Just relax,' he said and he got off the bed. He closed the curtains and took his clothes off. He went back to the bed. He lifted my skirt up and pulled my panties down. He kissed my foot everywhere and he said; 'This is already more leg than I know what to do with,' and he moved upwards. A hundred kisses further he was there and my eyes widened as a quivery moan escaped from between my lips. His finger went in and he was gently rubbing the inside of my pussy while he sucked on my clit. I took off my shirt and bra and he kept going. A glorious few minutes later, I came, and he heard, and I think Buck must also have heard but I didn't give a fuck about Buck. Vincent went further up and a hundred-and-fifty kisses and licks later he reached my mouth, and he wanted to kiss me but I said: 'Why don't you have a sport-life first?' He gave me a sweet evil grin and put his forehead against mine and I felt his cold breath on my lips and I wanted to kiss him but I didn't. I felt him move in there with his big pale dick. Pain had never hurt so good. I came again while we were fucking and then I did kiss him. He wasn't done fucking me after I came and he went on for a good five minutes before he got off and I could relax the pussy-muscles. He put his arm around me and he gave me the most loving smile and he licked my lips and nose and I smiled and I started laughing and he started laughing and then Doggio barked. It was like an air alarm had gone off. You could feel the floor vibrate for half-a-second after that bark. Buck came running down the stairs. Doggio sat down and looked very calmly at Buck. Buck looked as us.

'So, you kids fuck?'

'We make love,' Vincent said.

'Was that your dog?!'

'Yes. He wanted to celibate the love Sam and I just made. That's all.'

'Is he going to do that again?'

'Sam… what's that on your tit?'

'I don't see anything on her tit,' Buck said and then he said: 'Why the fuck am I looking at my little cousin's tits? Jesus. I'll leave you kids to it then… Can you hang a cowboy-hat on the door next time?'

'A cowboy-hat on the door?' I asked.

'Yes. That's how we always did it in good old Texas. Vince can you look at me? I know she has nice tits but… what the fuck am I saying! I'll get you kids a cowboy-hat later. And don't get pregnant on me Sam!' he said and then he closed the door of the living room.

'Sweet Sammie, you have my sincere compliments regarding your perky tits. Lemmy Kilmister,' Vincent read and then he rolled over the ground laughing. 'Did you… did you…' he said, trying to catch his breath, 'Did you lose your virginity to the ghost of Lemmy Kilmister?!'

'Yes!' I said.

'It doesn't count.'

'Why not?'

'Because ghosts aren't real. Everybody knows that!'

I started laughing too. That was really funny.

'Come on,' Vincent said, 'Let's get dressed and cool off outside with Doggio huh? Smoke some of that ganga-ganga.'

'Great idea Vince,' I said and not that much later I was wheeled threw the summer-night under the Colorado stars. There was a little park in the center of Dead Rat and he laid me down on the grass there, laid next to me and rolled a joint. 'Without the starlight in your eyes the world would be the darkest place,' he said.

'What's the point of light if it can't make me see you smile?'

'But you see me smile Sam. You'll always see me smile if you stay with me…'

'Did you smile when you brought me to hell?'

'I did Sam, and I'm sorry. But how could you know you're in heaven if you've never seen hell?'

'Where does this end Vincent?' I asked. I was scared.

'We'll know when we're dead,' Vincent whispered in my ear and then he kissed that ear. I was looking up at that infinity there. I wanted that.

'Only in your eyes and this sky above me do I see infinity,' I said.

'That is my infinite love for you, that you see.'

Shit, I thought, why does he always have to romance top me?! I thought and said: 'I fuck your dad.'

'I love you too,' he said and after that we just sort of laid there. Doggio put his head on my belly, and it was warm and soft but heavy as a bowling ball. And the stars shun on but we could never last. Then, suddenly, there was a noise, it was Vincent´s voice but his lips weren't moving. 'Whatever you were waiting for is ready,' the voice said. Vincent got his phone out of his pocked, 'Pizza's ready in ten minutes,' he said. 'These things are fucking convenient, you hungry Sam?'

'I could eat a horse!'

'Let's get you back in the chair then and make a run for it,' he said and he put me in the wheelchair and started running with it incredibly fast. I felt the wind in my hair. Doggio ran besides us. We were home in five minutes and it was a twenty-minute walk. I just laughed the entire way back.

Buck was beating the dough. We saw him fighting it in the window. He punched it as if that dough had killed his mother before his eyes. We came in the hall and he didn't notice us. 'You fucking dough! You die! You die you fucking dough! I am going to kill you! It's your fucking fault you stupid dough! *Killzio and Killziet* was a genius novel! You fucking dough! It's your fault! Prepare to be made a pizza of!'

We listened to it laughing, then we came into the room.

'Hi kids. Pizza will be ready in twenty minutes. Next time I'll show you how to do the rest of the pizza but I'm hungry and I want it done fast. Have you been running Vincent?'

'Yes, I took Sam for a run. I first saw her in the forest. She was running. I've been running after her ever since.'

'I can't wait until we can run together,' I said.

'You kids make me noxious. Remind me to take refuge in Siberia when Valentine's day arrives,' Buck said while he was rolling the dough and spun it in the air. He started putting all sorts of vegetables, spices, meat, cheeses and tomatoes on there. It smelled delicious. 'You haven't got a nice single mom do you Vincent?' Buck asked.

'I do,' Vincent said, 'but she's single for a reason.'

'And what reason might that be?'

'She's dead.'

'I'm sorry to hear that Vincent,' Buck said. He stopped with the pizza while he said that and he looked down. Then he did the last touches of the pizza and walked with it to the kitchen. 'You should visit me in Fresno, I've got a real stone oven there. Out of real stones. I could also make an oven out of you because you kids are really stoned, aren't you?'

'Yes,' Vincent and me said simultaneously.

'That's cool. Makes the pizza taste even better. I'm really glad you're cool kids. I was worried that you might be a bunch of imbeciles.'

'Most kids are imbeciles,' I said.

'Grown-ups are even worse.' Buck said, 'It's why most kids are imbeciles, it's because most adults are too. Where do you think they learn it from?'

Vincent put me on the couch and put my leg on the coffee table.

'He kids, I'm gonna smoke a joint too while the pizza's burning because I don't feel like eating pizza with stoned people while not being stoned myself. IF WE MUST BE STONED! LET US GET STONED TOGHETTER! AND THOU WITHOUT SIN CAN CAST THE FIRST STONE AND STONE US FURTHER!'

'You want some of mine?' Vincent asked.

'What kind?'

'I grew red devils in the mountains. I went up there a month ago and I saw a bee sitting on one of m', and when the bee got off, he sat right on the palm of my hand, totally relaxed and fell asleep.'

Bullshit, Buck said.

'Smell for yourself,' Vincent said and he held a big weed-bag open in front of Buck's nose.

'Well, well, well...' Buck said, 'You do understand that as a responsible adult, I do have to confiscate a substantial portion of that illegal substance you put your life in danger with,' and he got an empty click-bag off the table and held it in front of Vincent, who put a large chunk of marijuana in there. 'I'll be outside doing my own little romance thing with sweet Mary-Jane then,' he said and walked into the back garden.

Vincent got up, tapped on his phone and he put on the Motörhead album *Overnight Sensation*. He started dancing a little to it. Fifteen minutes later, Buck came in with a wide smile, red eyes and a big ass pizza. It smelled fucking delicious. He put the pizza on the table and opened a black wooden box. He took out a silver pizza-cutter. 'That's a real sixteen karat pizza-cutter there. I won that in Boston. I never leave my house without it. When some fucking motherfucker is gonna rob me, I'll pull this motherfucker on him and make a fucking sliced pizza out of that motherfucker! I tells you sweeties. I tells you! I motherfucking tells you sweet motherfuckers that if some motherfucker fucks with this motherfucker, I'm gonna motherfucking slice that motherfucker up with a motherfucking sixteen karate silver pizza-cutter! Shit... You kids want big or small slices?'

'Big slices!'

'I shall slice only three!'

'What about Doggio?' I asked.

'FOUR SLICES! Come here Doggio!'

Doggio did nothing. Vincent clicked with his mouth and Doggio got up right away and sat before us. Vincent put one of the huge pizza slices on its head. He waited five seconds, then he nodded and Doggio threw the slice in the air, caught it and ate it up it in one swallow.

'What the fuck kind of dog is that?' Buck asked.

'A very special breed.'

'What breed?'

'The breed that is MY DOG!'

'MY DOG!' I screamed.

'MY DAWG!' Buck screamed.

'DOG MY DAWG!' Vincent screamed and then Doggio howled and again the floor vibrated. The howl lasted three seconds and it was like all the orchestras in the world were playing together in the throat of that dog. 'Jesus,' Buck said and then we had the pizza.

'You kids like my pizza?' Buck asked.

'I would describe it as such;' I said, 'if God was a woman and the oven from which it came was her pussy, it'd be something like that pizza of yours.'

'Thanks. I also make pretty good omelets. And your dad's insurance gave me a big ass food budget. That's one good thing about working with big fucking corporate conglomerates. You get big fucking insurance. Everything is big in those big fucking things. Even the fucking is big. They'll fuck you big. They're big fuckers.'

'These slices are too,' I said.

'Yeah,' Vincent said, 'these are big fucking slices,' and then we just ate and listened to the Motörhead album that was still playing. 'I DON'T BELIEVE A WORD!' Lemmy sang. We had some wine after that and cigarettes outside. We didn't talk. Doggio said nothing. The stars said nothing. The wine said nothing. I said nothing. And then I said: 'What?'

'What, what?' Vince said.

'What, what, what?' Buck said.

'Nothing,' I said.

'I'm going to bed,' Buck said, 'Were you planning to go to school or something while I look after you?'

'I don't know. I'll think about it tomorrow.'

'Alright Sam, see you tomorrow.'

'You have a really nice uncle Sam,' Vincent said with a very wide smile and after we were done laughing about that he said: 'You look tired Sam.'

'I am,' I said and he wheeled me down to the living-room and put me in the bed. 'I'll be here shortly. I have to think about certain things alone for a few minutes.'

'Alright Vince.'

'Goodnight Sam.'

'Goodnight Vince.'

I was really tired from all this and I fell asleep shortly after. When I woke up and opened the curtains to the back yard, I saw Vincent still sitting there, with a notebook, a pen, a coffee and a joint, looking straight ahead. Doggio was sleeping in front of him.

6, Thunder

I have blood-type A-positive. So, when I take the pill, I have an increased risk of getting Thromboses by 80 percent. Nobody told me this. I had to look it up myself. I figured that I'd rather have a kid than Thromboses so I don't take them but I do have a morning-after pill in my wallet. I had never taken one before but I heard they make you noxious for a few hours. That's just worth not having to use a condom to me. So, when Buck came in with some Juice 'd Orange and mango, I wanted to take it right away. But when I was about to the put it in my mouth, I felt awful all the sudden, like all life had been taken out of life, like there was no hope. It hit me like a hammer, that feeling.

'Are you alright Sam?' Buck asked.

'Buck I...'

'Sam... Sam.... Sam?'

I saw Lemmy, leaning over my father's Harley with a bottle of Jack in his hand. Behind him was a sunset over the Himalayas. He looked at me in the twilight and lit a smoke. 'You thought life was so great huh Darling? If it's so great, then give it to my unborn child.'

'I'm... I'm carrying your baby?'

Lemmy got of the death-Harley and walked towards me, he drank the remaining half of the bottle in one gulp and threw it against a tree. He stood behind me and held his hand on my belly. 'Little boy in there. You know something darling, what you and me have is very special. Out on the earth you know, I am human and maybe a little too much of that but here...'

'Lemmy is God. The rumors are true,' I whispered.

'So, you see it's kind of important that kid inside of you finds its way out in one piece.'

'My child is Jesus...'

'No darling, I tried that. This is another prophet, the one they have all been asking for: Barabbas.'

'Barabbas...'

'You will say the father is not known to you and give it your name; Barabbas Breadmaker.'

'But they'll think I'm a total slut!'

Lemmy grunted. It scared the living shit out of me. He walked around me and got a mirror out of the saddle bag of the bike and held it up to my face 'SLUT' it said on my forehead.

'You will see this always, and so will everybody else if you question me ever again!'

'I'm sorry God,' I said.

'Call me Lemmy,' Lemmy said. He pretended to shoot me with his thumb and index finger and that zapped me back to where I lost myself.

'Sam? Sam? There you are. You went out for a second there. Is that anything I should worry about?'

'No, I just hate mornings.'

'It's almost afternoon.'

'Then you really don't have to worry about it,' I said but my voice started shaking at the end of the sentence.

'What's wrong Sam?' Buck asked as he put his hand on my shoulder.

'I'm pregnant!'

'Does Vincent know?'

'It's not Vince's.'

'Who's is it?'

'Mine.'

'You impregnated yourself?'

'I kind of did!'

'You don't know who it is?'

'No.'

'Where did it happen?'

'In the hospital.'

'Sam, we have to find out who it is...'

'No, we don't Buck. I don't want him to have anything to do with my baby. I don't even know his last name. He was a terminal patient. A young boy who begged me because he didn't want to die a virgin. I let him fuck me out of pity.'

'Well Sam, it's your life. But if you want my advice I...'

'...L ask for it.'

'OK, but either get it out or quit smoking. If I catch you smoking, I'll abort it myself you understand. Life is a beautiful thing Sam, but it´s not easy and if you don't do your absolute best for it you could end up destroying the most beautiful thing in this cold and empty bullshit we seem to float around in and you'll never forgive yourself. Trust me, I know. So, you don't drink, you don't smoke or get high and you don't eat any fucking red M&M's is that understood?' -I nodded- 'And we go to a doctor tomorrow. I promise I won't tell anybody OK.'

'OK Buck,' I said and a tear rolled down my face. Vincent came in with Doggio. Doggio sat down on the carpet and looked at me, holding his head in an angle. 'It's a beautiful sunny day and we've slept the half of it away!' Vincent sang.

Buck looked at me. "Tell him." said that look and then he went outside for a smoke.

'I want to get out of here Vincent,' I said.

'I'll take you somewhere special.'

'Where?'

'School.'

'I don't want to go to school anymore.'

'Trust me, you do. OK, maybe not today but tomorrow we go, and it'll just be one week and then it's summer break.'

'So, who cares?'

'I do, for all sorts of reasons.'

'Yeah, and what are those?'

'Let's go to the mountains today. I have a lot to explain and you must have a lot to ask. Where the air is the freshest the thinking is most clear. I have friends there I want to introduce you to.'

'That be nice.'

'You look like you can use some mountain air anyways. I'm gonna take a shower, you should take one too, oh wait, that'll be a little difficult. How do you do that?'

'Sponge.'

'We'll, the weather is great so why don't we take a carwash-shower? I'll just put some garbage bags over your leg and it'll be fine.'

'What?'

'I'll show you, come on,' he said and then he said: 'Buck we're leaving, we'll probably be back tomorrow before dusk and we'll let you know if it's going to be later.'

'OK,' said Buck and we were off.

I found out what a carwash-shower was in the carwash. It just means you put a coin in the machine, strip down to your underwear and hose each other down until the staff starts yelling at you and then you get back in the car and drive away fast. I had a lot of fun doing it. Vincent stopped somewhere in an ally and we got our clothes back on.

He put me back in the backseat of his Lexus and Doggio, who also had a good carwash-shower and was dried off the best we could sat next to him on the passenger's seat. Mozart's 40st was playing. 'It's my favorite Mozart symphony,' Vincent said.

'Mine is the 23'd,' I said.

'Also, Stalin's favorite.'

'Really?'

'Yes. The musicians that were ordered to play it for him were too nervous to play at first but in the end, Stalin was very pleased with the recording. I have it on CD here. You want to hear the terrified musicians play Mozart for Stalin?'

'MOZART FOR STALIN!' I screamed.

'MOZART FOR STALIN FOR YOU!'

'MOZART FOR STALIN FOR US!'

He got a CD out of his clove box and changed the CD in the stereo. And there was the 23'd, and I didn't hear the fear at all.

'I play the violin and have goosebumps on my skin!' I sang along with the music.

'Stalin's iron eye makes me freeze from within!'

'The fear is in my toes, the fear is in my nose, I can only lose here, I can never win!'

'The fear I can't sustain, his gaze is in my brain, the great comrade Stalin!'

'And the fear is in my eyes and the fear is in my chin, I hope he doesn't hear the fear...'

'OK on one. Three... two... one...'

'IN MY VIOLIN!' Vincent and me sang simultaneously to the sound of the musicians that actually felt this way. We drove on.

'I'm going to pick up a friend of mine: Wandering Eagle. He has been to many places and he has seen many things.'

'Is he also a vampire?'

'No. Nobody is a vampire. You shouldn't use that word. It's like calling a black person a nigger.'

'But you call us bloodcows!'

'Yeah but like... never mind, I'll school you on some mythical history later and you'll understand.'

'Oh yeah, the slave trade of the bronze age by the people you milk for blood.'

'You think you know something about anything about that?' Vincent said. He was really offended.

'Let's not argue Vince. It's a beautiful day.'

'You're right... Wandering Eagle said he would meet me on this road,' he said as he turned the music off and the car into a dirt road that went into the forest. Vincent started driving slowly again.

The road seemed to go on forever, cornering up besides cliffs and waterfalls and then we went over an old abandoned train-track. There was a tunnel. 'DO NOT ENTER! TUNNEL MIGHT COLLAPSE' said a sign in front of the tunnel. Vincent stopped before it, got out of the car and put the sign on the side of the tracks, then he drove the car into the tunnel, put the sign back and drove on. It was quite a long tunnel and we couldn't see further than the headlights for a while until there was light, and then there was a wooden bridge, over a stream crawling down to a lake two-hundred feet below. They had lain two rows of planks on the steel of the old train-track and tight them down with rope. On the other side of the bridge stood a big man, with a thick beard, long hair and a guitar on his back. There was something sad about him.

'I don't know about this bridge Vincent.'

'It's made by the Katanga. When they make something, it will always hold.'

'Who are the Katanga?' I asked Vincent, who was driving very slowly over the planks. He didn't answer and I decided that I didn't want to distract him further from what he was doing. When he was over the bridge, he stopped the car, got out and walked up to Wandering Eagle. I could hear what they said because the windows were open.

'My good friend Jumping with Deers. I am happy to see you,' Wandering Eagle said.

'I feel the same Wandering Eagle. Very much the same.'

'So, this is the woman that choose you?'

'Yes.'

'And you have also chosen her?'

'Yes.'

'I will meet her then,' he said and he walked up to the car. He opened the rear passenger door my back wasn't against and stuck his hand out to me. 'I am Wandering Eagle. It is an honor to meet you.'

'I am Sam,' I said, 'and the honor is all mine.'

'Don't take all the honor.'

'I'm sorry. I didn't mean to.'

'You are only young. In the future you will learn not to say things you don't mean. Things you don't mean are meaningless.'

'Are you guys Native Americans?'

'Please do not call us that. It are really stupid words. We are Indions.'

'Indions?'

'Yes. In Dio. People of God. It's what Columbus called us.'

'So, Vincent's Indian, I mean Indion name is Jumping with Deers?'

'Yes, what about it?'

'It's kind of a funny Indion name.'

'Not everybody can be Dancing with Wolves Sam.'

'Can I be Dancing with Wolves?'

'That's for the wolves to decide. But we will make talk later. You must drive further into the forest Jumping with Deers. I will sit on the roof.'

'You'll sit on the roof?!' I asked.

'Yes.' Wandering Eagle said and then Doggio made a very soft and low noise. 'I think your friend wants to sit on the roof too Jumping with Deers.'

'Alright then, take place and we go further into the forest,' Vincent said and he opened the passenger door. With one jump, Doggio was on the roof of the Lexus. Wandering Eagle climbed on there too. I saw it dent in pretty far. 'This is going to cost me my roof,' Vincent said.

'Cool,' I said, 'we'll make a convertible.'

'That's stupid.'

'It might seem crazy what I'm about to say...'

'What are you going to say Sam? It can't be that crazy.'

'Sunshine she's here, you can take a break?' you don't know this?

'We can't take a break we have to see the Katanga.'

'I'm a hot air-balloon that could go to space...'

'Sam, I have no idea what in the hell you are talking about.'

'With an air, like I don't care baby by the way?'

'What is it Sam?'

'BECAUSE I'M.... happy clap along if you feel like a car without a roof!' Wandering Eagle, who was still on the roof, started clapping right away when he heard me sing that and he sang along right away when he heard the lyric "Sing along if you feel like a car without a roof!" He started strumming his guitar, and we sang the chorus over and over through the mountain forest like that. Vincent was very annoyed by this. He didn't sing along. When my throat was sore from singing, Wandering Eagle said: 'We must not sing anymore. It might upset the forest. There is much time for music later,' and we were all quiet for a while.

Two men were waiting on the dead end of the train tracks. Doggio and Wandering Eagle got off the roof, Vincent got out and they approached them.

'Kiki OE,' One of the Indions said. Wandering Eagle nodded.

'What is he saying?' Vincent asked.

'He said that if we hurry, we will be on time to help with the fire. Come on, let's get your woman out of the car.'

They opened the door. 'Leave your phone in the car, it is not our way,' Wandering Eagle said and I put my phone on the back seat before they lifted me out of the car with extreme ease. They put me on a self-made stretcher, that was made out of rope, sticks and leaves. There were six dead rabbits tight to the branches. It was soft as a daisy. They started wrapping all sorts of animal skins around me. 'The beaver skin will protect you,' Wandering Eagle said and then they very tightly put a layer of rope around it all. They did it incredibly fast, without the slightest hesitation in their movements. When they were done, I could move nothing from the neck down. They lifted the stretcher up, put it on their shoulders and ran with it into the forest. I heard Vincent running behind me. Doggio and Wandering Eagle ran ahead. They jumped over logs and ran through streams. Wandering Eagle was making very strange and very beautiful music on his guitar while we were running. It was like he was playing in all the keys at the same time.

'He plays so the bears know it's them,' Vincent said with heavy runners' breath. After half-an-hour of this, we reached the entrance of a cave that was just narrow enough for one person to walk through at the time.

'Kariki Da,' the man that was holding the front of my stretcher said. Wandering Eagle nodded and grabbed a stick off the ground. He got some dried grass out of his pocked and wrapped it around it. With two fire-stones he had it on fire in two seconds.

'It is so the snakes know it is us. They are not our way,' Wandering Eagle said, and with the guitar on his back he walked into the cave. The rest followed behind. I heard a stream in the darkness. We went through a very complicated labyrinth of cave tunnels until suddenly, there was a blinding light. Wandering Eagle put out the torch in the sand and stuck the grass he had tight around it back in one of his pockets.

'Kiki Di,' said one of the Indions.

'What did he say?' I asked Wandering Eagle.

'He said: "Good, they have already made the fire, they did not need our help anyways", now let's bring Sam to Waking Dove. She will know.'

'Just trust these people Sam. They have lived here long before anybody else and they know a lot more about medicine than the doctors do. I'll help them skin the rabbits on your stretcher for the party and you listen very carefully to whatever Waking Dove says to you OK? Just keep an open mind.'

'If my mind wouldn't be open you wouldn't be in it.'

'That's true,' Vincent said. Wandering Eagle nodded. Then the men carried me away. I looked around and saw that I was still underground but there was a great hole in the rocks where the sun shone through. Everywhere were naked people. Kids, old ladies, young men, teenage girls... and they were all doing something. Some were making things, some were talking, some were making strange music on strange instruments with each other that echoed through the cave. And I couldn't help it, I started singing. I just had to know how it sounded there. I didn't sing any words, just the letter A in high tones and suddenly, someone started singing with me, and more people and more and then everybody was singing. They kept on going when the men carried me into another cave opening on the other side of the open place and one of them put his finger to my lips. They also stopped singing and very slowly walked down the tunnel.

Some skins were hung on the walls and there were all sorts of drawings of people hunting and animals. They went through a curtain of elk skins and I smelled the strangest smell I had ever smelled in my entire life. Like if the greatest bakery in the world had a location in a Buddhist temple next to a psychedelic hippie dungeon. And I heard a young, light, cheerful and very pleasant voice: 'Sam, I am Waking Dove. Don't be afraid. I learned to speak your language. Wandering Eagle taught me,' Then she said 'Karabus.' and the Indions put me down by the small fire that was burning in the cave. The smoke could easily get out because the room was much lower than the entrance. The Indions that carried me in undid the ropes and went out of the room. 'First I must undress you. Is that OK? You see, I am naked too so there is nothing to fear.'

'OK,' I said and I smiled and I looked at her. She must have been somewhere in her early twenties and she was the most stunning woman I had ever seen. Her eyes were black, wide and enigmatic, long black brads fell over curvy cheeks and her mouth seemed to open and close like a flower. 'What is this metal on your teeth?' she asked after she undressed me fully and put two fingers on my forehead, gently pressing it downwards. 'Don't worry about it,' I said. 'It is not your way.' She then stroked her fingers over my nose, my lips, chin, neck, in between my breast and over my belly. She put her hand firmly on my head and looked at me with intense emotion of all kinds. A tear dropped out of her eye and fell into mine. 'I see...' she said.

'What did you see?' I asked.

More tears started appearing in her eyes but she never took them off mine. 'Everything.' she whispered and she put her hand on my belly. 'HA!' she screamed loudly and jumped up. She got a bunch of gigantic leaves out of the corner of the room and waved them over the fire. 'HA! HA! HA!' she yelled and she sat down before me. 'Eat,' she said and she held her hand palm up to me. There were small blue mushrooms in her hand. I looked at it hesitantly. 'Do not worry. The child shall not be harmed,' she said. I ate the mushrooms. They tasted awful. Waking Dove started eating them too. 'We will see what the fire tells us,' she said. She looked to the wall for a second or two and she said: 'While we wait for the holy plant to show us, I shall fix your leg, is that OK?'

'Yes,' I said.

Walking Dove picked up a very big and very sharp looking knife out of nowhere and started cutting the casket loose.

'Should you do that? The doctor said...'

'How can I fix your leg if it is in a casket?' Waking Dove said and she kept on cutting the casket. It was off there in less than twenty seconds. There were two parts of it left. 'Take this back to your world for it does not belong in ours,' she said, holding the two parts of the casket. My left leg, that was once half my pride and glory was now thin and pale. Very gently, Walking Dove smeared some sort of very strongly smelling potion on it that had a very tingling feeling to it. 'There is a stick Sam. And you're going to get the stick.'

'What?!'

'A stick. You're going to get the stick,' she said and she got a stick from beneath a bunch of animal hides. There were all sorts of things carved in the stick. 'I saw in a vision that I needed this stick. Now it is dry and ready. Look, it fits perfectly with your bones,' she said as she held the stick next to my leg. She got some sort of rope and she rolled it around my leg in a strange crossway motion until my entire leg was covered with rope. 'You can take it off the day after tomorrow. Then wait two days and you can run and jump again. And keep the rope and the stick. It is my gift to you young Sam,' she said with a loving smile.

'But the doctor said I have to spend at least another...'

'Then he is not a very good doctor,' she said, 'Let's look in the fire, shall we? The spirits will show us what we *need* to know. They never show what we *want* to know. So never look for what you *want* to know but look for what you *need* to know.'

'OK,' I said and I stared into the fire. I saw nothing but fire. Then I heard thunder.

'Gori Ki,' Walking Dove said.

'What does that mean?' I asked.

'It means the BBQ is off. But it also means the spirit of the thunder might come to see us.'

'The spirit of the thunder?'

'Yes Sam. There is an old Indion song that we sing to summon the spirit of the thunder. I will sing it for you: 'AHAHAHAHAHAHOW!'

'I know that song!' I said, enthusiastic beyond believe.

'You know our ancient songs?'

'But that's ACDC!'

'No, the spirit of the tides is a completely different song.'

'No, the band ACDC! They made a song called Thunderstruck and it's exactly the same!'

'Let's sing it then,' Waking Dove said and then she screamed 'AHAHAHAHAHAHOW!' seven times, frantically into the fire and looked at me...

'THUNDER!' I screamed even more frantically into the fire.

'AHAHAHAHAHAHOW!'

'THUNDER!'

'AHAHAHAHAHAHOW!'

'THUNDER!'

'AHAHAHAHAHAHOW!'

'THUNDER!'

'AHAHAHAHAHAHOW!'

'THUNDER!'

'AHAHAHAHAHAHOW!'

'THUNDER!'

'AHAHAHAHAHAHOW!'

'THUNDER!'

'Yeah!'

And then we simultaneously screamed the rest of that song into the fire. She in her language and I in mine. When the song of Thunderstruck came to an ending, three strucks of thunder where heard. I saw wolves in the fire. I looked at Waking Dove, who was looking at the fire with intense interest. She looked at me and she nodded. I saw myself in the fire. I was in the forest, naked. I looked at Waking Dove again. She nodded again towards the fire. Five wolves jumped in front of me. The white wolf started running. I ran after it and the rest ran behind us. We just ran through the forest.

'Hmmm. That was the first thing the fire had to tell you of course.'

'What is that?'

'Your spirit-name.'

I looked at the fire again. I grinned very widely at the fire. 'O yes,' I said.

'What do you mean?'

'I mean... that is so fucking cool... the spirit of the thunder tells me I'm...'

'Running with Wolves, yes? But I don't understand... how is that cool? Running makes you hot and thunder makes fire that is also hot.'

'I'm pretty fucking hot then am I not Waking Dove?'

'I would say you are, yes. But look into the fire. The spirit of the thunder must have much more to tell us,' and we looked at the fire. I saw myself trip over a rat, one of the wolves (the white one) came to help me and the rat bit it's throat and killed it. Then I saw a red one rip the rat in two and I ran further with rest of the pack. I just kept on running in the fire.

'Listen?' Waking Dove said, 'The spirit is making music with the fire. It is an instrument not of this world. I have heard it once before. It is the instrument of the thunder. Do you hear it?'

'That's an electric guitar,' I said.

'How do you know about this instrument of thunder?'

'I play one,' I said, 'I don't like to brag about it but I'm pretty good.'

'Can you bring one next time? I would like to see it. Or is it dangerous to show it?'

'No, it's not. But you can't play it here because you need a machine that catches the thunder and those machines are dangerous.'

'Dangerous how?'

'I don't think you want to know,' I said.

'I don't think so either. But let's just listen to this strange music that the spirit of the thunder is making for you,' she said as the highly pitched and heavily distorted guitar played something within a harmonic D minor scale with a lot of tapping and pull offs. It had the low E string dropped to a D, something I like to do too and was picking four beats somewhere around 130 BPM. The spirit of the thunder also went hard on the fuzz pedal. I told Waking Dove: 'Can you tell Wandering Eagle that the spirit of the thunder wants to rock with Running with Wolves?' She nodded and left the cave. I kept on listening to that spirit in the fire. I saw a red wolf playing a Gibson Gold top.

Waking Dove rushed in with Wandering Eagle's acoustic guitar. There was no brand name on it or nothing but there were all sorts of wild animals carved into it. The bridge was nice and low and he used light strings which I also liked.

'Wandering Eagle said he understood. He wishes much wisdom will fall upon you in the act of rocking with the spirit of the thunder. Here, have this. It is to be used only by those that make music with the spirits. It is very old. It is called Takana Karika, it means...'

'You have to be kidding me!'

'Why? What is wrong Running with Wolves? It is very old, it means…' she said as she held the old green wooden plectrum shaped the EXACT same way as in that fucking movie in front of me.

'The pick of destiny.'

'You are very strange are you not young Running with Wolves?'

'I am,' I said while I dropped the E down. The red wolf stopped playing so I could tune.

The moment I hit the first note of a lick that could lick the fire, a band appeared behind it. A band of wolves. A white one on the drums, a black one bass and a gray one was howling. There was this amazing riff in E-pentatonic and I came up with all sorts of cool stuff over it. It wasn't an easy riff and I hadn't played in months because my mom took my guitar away because "I could not learn what a volume knob is for so I just had to play with the volume knob without the guitar for a while" I turned the amp up full volume and drummed with my index finger on the jack right after she left. She came in shortly after that and also took my amp away. But it felt so natural. I figured the chords out in a manner of minutes. I played until my fingers bled. Then I played more. I just screamed at the fire to make the pain go away. Waking Dove was sitting in the corner of the room and she smoked something out of a pipe. The fretboard became red with blood. Very calmly, Waking Dove moved out of the cave. A bowl of water was thrown on the fire. 'It's enough Running with Wolves,' Waking Dove said, holding the empty bowl and she sat down in front of me with open palms. I handed her the guitar. 'Rest,' she said and again she put my head down on the soft animal skins. She closed my eyes with her fingers and I did not open them, not because I was afraid to open them but simply because I didn't want to. I slept the blackest sleep. When I woke up, Vincent and Doggio were lying next to me.

'You got a cool Indion name?' he asked, 'Waking Dove felt like you would like to tell it yourself.'

'Running with wolves,' I said with the proudest grin.

'You have to be kidding me!'

'Nope.'

'Well, when they hunt me down, I rather jump over the hurdle than turn around and show my teeth. Here, try this; Wandering Eagle gave me this. It's great natural tobacco,' he said as he started stuffing a self-made wooden pipe.

'I'm pregnant Vince,' I said.

'That's impossible. I gave myself a Vasectomy.'

'What?!'

'It's an easy operation. You can use acupuncture to block certain nerve centers from responding and then you...'

'I don't want to hear about that Vince... You really did this?'

'Yes. I can reverse it any time I want. Maybe you were just noxious from the wine this morning?'

'But it's not yours!

'O NO SAM!' he said and he lifted his hands to the ceiling in complete desperation.

'Vince,' I said and I pointed at my left tit.

'Jesus,'

'No,' I said, 'Barabbas,' and Doggio gently put his paw on my naked belly and made a soft low sound.

7, Slut of the Future

It was as yet dull when we got up and there was a little fire consuming in the cavern opening. Meandering Eagle and Vincent conveyed me there on the cot. At the point when they put me down, Wandering Eagle left us there, without a word. Five young ladies came and began making tea on the fire. They gave us a cup. At the point when the tea was brought down, the morning nightfall began sparkling in from a higher place and I could see a few sparrows fly up to the opening. Meandering Eagle approached us and gave us hare meat.

'It is savvy to eat before your excursion,' he said.

'Much obliged to you, Wandering Eagle,' I said, 'and what is this venture you discuss?'

'Your excursion to school.'

'Better believe it, after this hare we truly need to get rolling. We'll be late for math since it's now five AM I actually need to drop off Doggio at home.'

'My supplements on the cooking coincidentally,' I said to Wandering Eagle.

'I will give the supplements to my grandma.'

'Did she cook it?'

'No, I did, however my grandma likes supplements better compared to me.'

'Goodness,' I said. I needed to toss the bones on the fire however Wandering Eagle said: 'Pause!' and he held his hand out to me. I gave him the bones and he put them in a pack that was looming behind him, 'I will get dressed and I will walk you and your lady to your vehicle,' he said, 'You get dressed too Sam. I realize they take a gander at you amusing in the event that you don't.'

'Indeed, they do.'

'I'll get your garments,' Vincent said and he left me by the fire with the young ladies. I paid attention to their language. Now and again there was a chuckle and a look towards me. Then, at that point, one of them checked out me straight and said: 'Thunder?'

'Ahahahahahahow,' I sang delicately and they all began chuckling once more. Vincent returned with my garments and just after I was finished getting dressed, Wandering Eagle and Vincent got the cot. Meandering Eagle drove the way through the caverns. We strolled gradually through the woods. It took us an hour to get to the vehicle. I didn't have the foggiest idea when school should begin yet I certain as poop wanted to miss a great deal of it. It just felt like such a disappointment to return to that spot.

'I have a werewolf to chase Sam,' Vincent said as we drove off.

'Do you have any idea what its identity is?'

'A werewolf follows up on frantic love. Assuming a werewolf is infatuated with somebody and that individual doesn't cherish them back, they could attempt to kill that individual. I believe it's Ann.'

'You think Ann is infatuated with you?'

'Indeed.'

'In any case, she loathes you!'

'That is the reason she's infatuated with me.'

'Extraordinary rationale. All in all, would that be able to happen to anyone, that werewolf thing?'

'At the point when you are chomped by one, or by a wolf that has been turned.'

'Like Doggio?'

'Doggio is unique. Just his mom was turned. You can't actually prepare a Beelzebat-Wolf however you can assuming you cross it with other canine varieties. I turned a wolf in bondage, reared with it and the outcome was Doggio.'

'Anyway, what befell his mom?'

'We needed to kill her. It would've been hazardous,' Vincent said. Doggio lifted up his lip for a negligible portion of a subsequent when he said that. Vincent didn't see this is on the grounds that he was checking out the street. I didn't enlighten him yet I contemplated whether perhaps Doggio comprehended.

'All in all, Annabel attempted to kill you?'

'Indeed... I think.'

'Does she have any familiarity with it?'

'Indeed. They recollect. They don't have a lot of command over how they are treating the thing goes. They just... depend on their instinct, I presume. Along these lines, they kill individuals that don't adore them back or individuals that are impeding them getting to their affection. It's franticness and they know it. However, they decide to change in any case.'

'They pick?'

'Indeed. They can't alter without putting their perspective to it. Takes about an hour for them to get into it. They need to plunk down and intentionally center around turning into a werewolf.'

'Also what might be said about the moon?'

'They love it.'

'However, do they require it?'

'No, they simply love it. They love to do it in that light for reasons unknown. Go around in a few twisted dream, butchering individuals in view of an infatuated heart.'

'Also you really want silver to kill them?'

'Solely after they change. Before the change they are similarly as simple to kill as you are.'

'I'm difficult to kill Vince. Lemmy said as much.'

'Please accept my apologies, I didn't intend to affront you, it's simply that the Bronze Kings are really...'

'Vincent?'

'Indeed?'

'It's a horrendous day. How about we contend.'

'What might be said about?'

'The word vampire.'

'If you don't mind, kindly not say that! I'll vow to quit calling you bloodcow on the off chance that you quit calling me... that fucking word OK?'

'I need to be your bloodcow Vince. Be that as it may, I likewise need you to be my vampire.'

'What sort of blood classification do you have at any rate?' Vincent asked as nonchalantly as possible.

'A-positive.'

His eyes broadened and his understudies became red. I saw long teeth arise out of the blue in his mouth. They were very white and he took a gander at me. The teeth looked unquestionably sharp and they twisted a little to the center of his mouth. Presently it wasn't only the students that were red any longer, it were his whole eyes!

'Vince it's me... kindly don't kill me...' I murmured in fear.

'I know Sam... it resembles... at the point when you check out somebody and you get an oopsy-daisy it doesn't mean you will assault her.'

'Thus, you need to tear into me more since I have A-positive?' Vincent began breathing intensely when I said that.

'You got a blade Vince?' I inquired.

'You need something to shield yourself from me? I see however that wouldn't work, you see B... vampires are...'

'No Vince... I simply need to provide you with a little taste of me. There's nothing more to it. I want to know what you think.'

'Of... of... what?'

'Of the manner in which my blood tastes sham!' I said. He halted the vehicle.

'I generally convey some stuff for side of the road medical procedure,' he said and he got out. He opened the storage compartment, got something out and sat on his knees before me toward the rear of the vehicle. He opened a pack with a wide range of extremely sharp surgical blades, forceps and god knows what.

'Are you certain you need to allow me to do this?' Vincent inquired.

'I'm certain,' I said, 'I realize that it is so essential to you.'

'Where do you need me to cut?'

'My butt. I need you to cut something sweet in there.'

'My god you are... you are the most astonishing bloodcowgirl in the fucking universe, you are...'

'Save it for my butt,' I said, and I pivoted.

He lifted my skirt up and pulled my undies down. The edge was sharp that it made the aggravation delicate. He was just bustling cutting for fifteen seconds. He cut something on my right butt cheek. I'm happy he didn't choose to begin a clever there. I felt the circulatory system down and his tong lick it off there, 'My sweet sky... this is so sweet... this is... mmmm!' Vincent said in the middle of his licking.

'You got a thing for A-positive?'

'Do I feel weak at the knees over A-good! Mmmm! Ahw... okay. That is sufficient now Vince. You don't want to drain her dry. This will consume a little Sam,' he said and it consumed a bit.

'What did you compose there?'

'You'll see later. It's a little shock. You'll adore it. We'll take the gauze off this evening.'

I pivoted. The remainder of the ride was somewhat less agreeable.

'Vince?' I asked not long before he pulled up before his home.

'Indeed?'

'Would you be able to transform into a bat?'

'No.'

'Great.'

'Would you be able to stand by in the vehicle? I would rather not convey you up this multitude of steps. I'm simply going to place Doggio in the house and get my books. There's nothing more to it. You need some espresso?'

'Indeed. Is it true that you will make those cappuccinos once more?'

'Okay,' he said and he got out. I saw him and Doggio stroll up that large number of steps. I really wanted a smoke. I saw Vincent's pack on the dashboard. He didn't smoke in the vehicle the whole ride. 'Lemmy, in the event that you don't need me to smoke, offer me hint,' I said and exactly when I said that, the sunscreen went down and something dropped out of its compartment. It was gold. It was one of those open and close lighters. 'Zippo' it read so those sorts, I presume. There was a Motörhead logo and Lemmy's face on it in dark. I lit the best smoke I at any point had. There's a great deal to say for the vampire-sentiment way of life yet it sure is unpleasant. I checked out the lighter while I was smoking. I checked out the back. 'Will you wed me?' said the rear of the zippo.

'O crap!' I said and I attempted to return it to the compartment however I was unable to arrive at it. I saw Vincent stroll down the steps and I immediately put the cigarette out in the debris train and waved my hand around to get the smoke out. I put the lighter in my pocket and I recently trusted that I would find an opportunity to return it there before he would see since I would have rather not screw this up for him. Likewise, I had a thought of how I could at last sentiment top Vincent now yet I must be speedy with regards to it.

'Think about what?' he said while he got in the vehicle and given me an espresso. He put the sunscreen up without checking out it.

'What?'

'Love-letter from Ann,' he said and he tossed a red envelope with a white heart on it at me.

'How would you know it's from Ann?'

'Since who might be so fucking style-less to stick a white heart you remove of a white paper on a red envelope with stick? The sort of individual that can't comprehend the Matrix.' he said as I opened the letter.

'Vincent. It's Ann,' I read.

'Isn't it obvious? Just read the rest while I fold this over your leg so they would look into your vampire sweetheart's mysterious Indion companions in the wild OK? It may crack them out a bit.'

I returned to perusing the letter.

You were so correct with regards to the Matrix. I didn't see any of it. I actually don't and I watched it multiple times since when you message me. I surmise I truly have down condition...

Please accept my apologies. It's simply that, I did some exploration on you since I sort of run this school in light of the fact that my father is the most extravagant man around and I like to know who the newbies are in Dead Rat. There aren't a large number. I have my methodologies and I discovered you were this chess player in Denmark and that you made like 1,000,000 in a game with some private bet or something and you drove a Ferrari and I resembled amazing! At long last, a person of my standard.

However at that point you got with that geek young lady Sam or something since you were modest or something yet I'm here Vince!!! I planned to say something yet I was simply pissed at Sam since she realizes I generally converse with the novices first. I wasn't attempting to insult you or anything. I don't have any idea where you went all of the unexpected yet I heard Sam was in a mishap. It's truly tragic sort of. Everyone is inquiring as to whether I need to get there or acquire my vehicle however like, it resembles as far as possible in fucking Denver and I don't need anyone to drive my vehicle since it's truly costly. It's that yellow Jeep. Have you seen it? You like it? We should like, absolutely drive in the mountains or something like that. Kindly call me Vincent. My number is on the back.

XX

Annabel.

'That bitch is an all out fucking werewolf,' I said after I wrapped up perusing the letter.

'We better kill her then, at that point,' Vincent said.

'You ought to have a little date with her in the mountains. And afterward you hold her down and I'll put a silver blade to her throat and I'll say that she's complete fucking twat and I'll cut her up like a fucking pizza.'

'Jesus Sam. Indeed, I surmise we could do that really, stand by, this letter is likewise significant. It's from Kharkanov.'

'That was Ghargatron's dad, right?'

'Indeed. The stamp is true so it must be.'

'Would you like to understand it?'

'Okay.' Vincent said and began perusing Kharkanov's letter

'The principal page simply says: "For battling valiantly on my child's side, I recognize you and give you his last letter to me. Best of luck with his question. I trust the execution of his will be a smooth operation."' then, at that point, he began perusing the following page of the letter.

Dear dad,

Two bitches have brought forth homes of six cups each. One lady has brought forth one young lady too. She will be a fine little girl. I have named her Petite, since she is little. The lady will go to live with her in Paris. I have incredible expectations for them.

Vincent has educated me regarding a young lady he enjoys. He isn't quick to like individuals so perhaps she is fit. I desire to find somebody soon so I don't need to choose from scramble. I asked him how he observed this young lady and he let me know that he was enlivened to go to a school of teaching by the shadow aces in the wake of seeing a film called "Twilight".

I have just seen three movies in my day to day existence: a film called "Birth of a nation.", a film called "Triumph of the Will" and a film called "Blackula". I preferred those films. I realized I would like them before I saw them in light of the fact that the titles were great. Yet, after "Blackula", I plainly expressed: 'There is no requirement for additional movies than the three movies I have seen. Everything is in these movies that can be communicated thanks to film. We find in the first the way that it ascends, in the second the way in which it falls and in the third the way in which it vindicates itself. The rest will be just reiteration of the equivalent essence.", however presently, after I knew about this film called "Twilight", I joyfully announce that I should withdraw that assertion for after it has risen, fallen and retaliated for itself, all that rests is for it is to end.

The film of "Twilight" is about numerous things, yet it is basically a severe Hegelian film. We search for evil, which is the dim, on the grounds that the second after we are conceived, the light damages our eyes and we can't see since it is excessively brilliant, yet when we arrive at the murkiness, we can't see either, for there is no light in the obscurity. Along these lines, we need to return to the light. Moving to and fro in the middle of a theory and a direct opposite is futile to no end can advance and that which doesn't advance will in general hold the future prisoner out of dread for the past. Life is the idea of compulsion, similarly as dependence is the idea of life. Enslavement is fascination with substance, and obviously, the general rule that good energy attracts good over-ranges al. Yet, presently take the well-known axiom from James Joyce: "Give substance to shadows.". The insight of how we can get away from our tendency as addicts to the light or the haziness isn't to be found more clear, and more justifiable than in the film of "Twilight", on the grounds that when a Hegelian methodology is taken towards building a similarity that embodies the pattern towards stagnation in involutionary development in the advanced human condition we see that as assuming this purported "evil" addresses restraint or hence, a shadow that isn't being adjusted as the new light yet is essentially given substance to, we could take this supposed "good", which is the light and make a combinations with it were we are protected, were we can walk, talk and sneak kisses: the nightfall.

Along these lines, I prescribe this film of "Twilight" to every individual who can hear, see or both in light of the fact that it has a decent title. We should see it together soon, will we father? I give you my favors to mother so you might give mother to my gifts.

Good tidings from your child Ghargatron, King of Kings.

P.S.

I have seen my demise. It will be a decent demise. My body will take care of the sharks. I feel it will happen soon. I will have my will prepared in three days for I dread I am right in continuously accepting I am correct. It will be in the vault. The person who enters the right mix will be compensated past their creative mind for they will be more extravagant than the most extravagant creative mind can envision. The person who enters it wrong will kick the bucket. The prediction will unfurl. The monster is coming. The hour of the wolf has arrived. Here is the conundrum that should be told to the Kings in case of my demise:

" I've worked at Auschwitz, multi week, besides on the master's day. Then, at that point, out of blanket I quit. After I went to chapel and asked, God advised me to go to the desert for 40 days and afterward He would excuse me.

I increased the days I worked in the camp until I was on schedule and in hours I left. At how time treated leave?"

Enter the code in the vault of my boat, the Gharnagan. Right blend brings fortune and wrong mix brings passing. You'll track down my will in my Bugatti. A King of Kings should live everlastingly after his passing and every other person's!

'O my God Vincent! Do you suppose Ann likewise killed that lady's child?'

'No,

'Peruse on then, at that point, and hopefully she's not unknown.'

'Or then again... he.'

'Screw Sam. I would rather not ponder that. Just read the letter.'

'I truly trust it's a person,' I said and I began perusing its remainder:

I'm so tired of it Vincent. I've been in this godforsaken spot for my entire life and thea'Read on then, and let's hope she's not anonymous.'

'Or... he.'

'Fuck Sam. I don't want to think about that. Just read the letter.'

'I really hope it's a guy,' I said and I started reading the rest of it:

I'm so sick of it Vincent. I've been in this godforsaken place all my life and the only light I could find I had to stick up my nose.

I stopped reading at that line. 'I know who it is,' I said.

'You're going to tell me it's a guy of course.'

'No, it's Susy, she's the school's cokewhore.'

'Well, nobody says cokewhores can't be werewolves. Read on.'

Every time I put my dad's gun in my mouth and sit in the darkness, a feeling that someday somebody will take me away from here and helps me live a life worth living stops me from pulling the trigger and help me god it will not be

that fucking "boyfriend" of mine. He treats me like garbage
and even beats me sometimes but he's very manipulative
and he keeps me hooked on the dope.

I was hoping maybe you would take me away from here,
because I found out what you are. I'm pretty fucking naive
Vincent, but I never thought that Twilight bullshit was
going to save me. But yeah, during lunch, I followed you to
your car the first day you were at school and I saw you
change and drink blood.

I love you Vincent, and if you don't love me, will you please
kill me and drink my blood because I can't change without
you and I can't keep on going this way. I would much rather
die as your vampire food than keep on living as Tygo's
sperm bucket.

My heart is yours, and so is the blood it is pumping,

Susy

Please call me, my number is on the back.

'Jesus,' Vincent said.

'That's the saddest thing I ever read.'

'Yeah, it's really sad.'

I stuck the letters in my pocket and we just looked at the
road, thinking of how sad it was.

After we drove out of the forest and were approaching town, I thought of something. 'You said werewolves change because they want to kill people out of mad love, right?'

'Yes.'

'So, what if Tygo found out Susy is in love with you? Would that not be a reason for him to turn if he was a werewolf?'

'You're right Sam,' Vincent said for the first time in this story.

'So, now we have four suspects.'

'It seems like it, yes.'

'Why do you have to be so fucking cute!' I said and I punched him on the shoulder. He laughed, 'Were you really a chess champion in Denmark?'

'Jed var Danmarks bedste,' he said as he drove the car into the parking-lot and got the wheelchair out of the trunk, 'I think we're on time for math,' he said, 'I checked the schedule. We both have math.'

'What's the point of school Vince? We already have their numbers and it's not like they aren't prepared to come to you. Just tell Susy to bring her boyfriend along so you can teach him a lesson and we'll find out who it is at your place. How do you find out actually?'

'You look them in the eyes and you can see if they lie when you ask them. Also, you can taste it but you have to drink a lot. And I won't teach that boyfriend of hers a lesson. I am going to kill him though, regardless if he is a werewolf or not.'

'I'd like to see that Vincent, but can we please not go to fucking math?'

'Alright Sam. We can just go to my place to Netflix and chill in the meantime. I've got a beamer,' he said and he put the wheelchair back in the trunk and drove off the parking-lot.

'Vince?' I said as we drove out into the street.

'What is it Sammie?'

'I have to tell you something.'

'What is it Sammie?'

'I never watched Twilight.'

'You haven´t missed much.'

'Vince?'

'Yeah?'

'Will you watch Twilight with me?'

'Alright Sammie. We've been through a lot but I think this will be our greatest adventure yet.'

'I think so too,' I said and I thought, 'Poor Susy.' and then I thought, 'Unless she's a werewolf.'

We couldn't get past the first ten minutes of Twilight so we just fucked on the couch. I couldn't believe the ease with which he had carried me up all those stairs. After a quick argument we decided that if it was Lemmy's baby I was carrying that some weed won't hurt it and so we got high, then we fucked again on the terrace outside and sat there for a while in silence. 'I'm going to call them,' Vincent said eventually. He took his phone out of his pocket and put it on speaker.

'Hello?'

'Annabel?'

'Who are you?'

'Vincent. I got your letter.'

'Vincent... Where were you? And what are you going to do?'

'I'm going to invite you over for dinner tonight. We can talk about it. Wear something sexy and classy. There will be more guest.'

'Who are they?'

'You'll see.'

'Are they rich?'

'Yes.'

'How late?'

'The dinner party is from seven till twelve at my house, then we'll decide if we want to turn it into another kind of party.'

'Alright. I'll be there,' she said and she made two kiss noises and was about to hang up but Vincent said: 'Wait!' and Ann said: 'What is it?'

'Something very important. If you plan to bring wine, I like red.'

'Alright Vincent,' she said and then Vincent hung up the phone. I smiled.

'OK, next suspect.'

'I need a smoke first,' Vincent said and he lit a cigarette. He dilled the number. We waited five seconds to that beep, before it went over.

'Please...' said a voice on the other side of the phone.

'It's Vincent Susy.'

'I'm... I'm... O my God.... I was about to... O my God...'

'Where are you Susy?'

'At... I'm at the old bridge Vincent.'

'Jesus. I'll pick you up. Just stay put and don't do anything crazy OK?'

'OK...' Susy said and she started crying.

'I'll be there in twenty minutes,' Vincent said and he hung up the phone. After Vincent left, I took my phone out of my pocket and designed and ordered my romance-top thing.

And just as that was done, Ann walked into the house. 'What are you doing here Sam?' she asked.

'What are you doing here? The party is at seven, didn't you hear?'

'Yeah, but what are you doing here?'

'I'm getting dead.'

'You're weird. Where's Vincent. I want to help him with the preparations. A dinner party is always better with a girl's touch I say. Good thing I came cuz you don't look like you could be of much help. I heard your dad's gay. And that he is in a coma or something. What is it Sam? Why do you look at me like that?'

'I just have PMS Annabel, don't worry about it.'

'Anyways, look what I brought: Vincent wine!' she said and she held a red bottle of Vincent wine in the air. 'It's really expensive. Good thing I have some class and know about these things,' she said as Vincent walked in the house with Susy, who had a black eye and a cut on her eyebrow.

'Vincent! There you are. What happened to you Susy?' Ann asked.

'I got drunk with Tygo last night and I fell against the toilet when I had to vomit. Then I had to vomit and I woke up in my blood and vomit.'

'You shouldn't drink so much Susy, you're already clumsy enough when you're sober.'

Vincent's eyes became red and his fangs started appearing.

'O.M.G.' Ann said, 'this is just like Twilight!'

'It's really nothing like in the movies.' I said and then Vincent bit her head off in one bite. He drank all of her blood straight from her neck as he held up her headless body as if it was a Coca Cola. She was drained and blue in less than ten seconds. He threw the headless blue bitch at Doggio and Doggio digested her even quicker than Vincent had drained her blood. Her cracking bones were the greatest music I had ever had the pleasure of listening to except for Motörhead. He put her head on the table. 'Call Tygo and invite him over for a dinner party,' he said to Susy, 'I think the moon is full tonight!' And he looked at me with the most terrifying grin that a stream of blood ever poured out of. 'Not bad,' he said to me, 'for a B-negative I mean.'

'Can… can you do it?' she said as she handed her phone to Vincent. She was shaking all over. It reminded me of the song Shaking all over.

'Give me the phone Susy. I'll call Tygo.' I said and Susy gave me the phone. It was already going over.

'Hi Tygo, it's Sam.'

'Hi sugar, why you callin' me on my girls' phone?'

'I'm getting high in the forest with Susy but she passed out. I think Vincent was also here just now. We really need some Angel Dust and a dick that's a little bigger than five inches. We're at Vincent's place. Everybody seems to know where that is for some reason so so should you. You gonna be there?'

'Yeah… Imma be there. How much dust you need?'

'How much you got?'

'More than you can ever effort biatch so just tell me what you need.'

'Five grams.'

'That's a hundo babe. You got a hundo?'

'I got a hundo. Can you be there in half?'

'Baby I be there in TEN! Get that pussy wet for me will ya?'

'You get that pussy wet yourself Tygo.'

'Ayt. I'm on my way back from Denver, I can be there in ten,' he said and he hung up the phone.

'Alright,' Vincent said, 'Susy can you wait in the kitchen for five minutes? There are some private things Sam and me have to discuss.'

Susy cried softly and left the living-room without a word.

'I don't think Ann is the werewolf. She didn't taste any different than the next B-negative bitch in the line for the bathroom. Now I'm going to kill Tygo and if I don't taste any in his blood you know what we have to do right?' he whispered.

'Jesus Vincent,' I whispered back, 'You don't think Susy would do that do you?'

'People are complicated Sam. The one thing I learned from studying brains is that you can never understand them.'

'Alright, but can I ask you one thing?'

'What is it?'

'Can I please be the one that kills Tygo?'

'Do you know how to use a gun?'

'Yes.'

'This isn't like with the Ferrari engine in my Lexus, right?'

'Give me your gun and I'll prove it.'

'OK,' Vincent said and he took off his 42 and ankle holster and put it around my ankle. 'Show me.'

'Can you make Ann face me?' I asked and Vincent turned Ann's head. I drew quick and shot straight through her right eye. Susy started screaming in the kitchen.

'You keep that! It's yours! You've earned it!' Vincent yelled proudly as he got up and knocked on the kitchen door. 'OK Susy, the matter is discussed and that shot was just for practice. Let's have a smoke and talk about what we are going to do.'

'Vincent I'm sorry... I... I have to be alone for a little while I can't look at this... I can't see this... What are you? What ARE you two? This is... I can't... You two are monsters!'

'Can I come in Susy?'

'No please.... I can't... I just... I can't fucking TAKE this shit anymore!' she said and then there was a shot. Vincent opened the door. I saw her lying on the floor. She had blown her own brains out.

Through the class, I saw Tygo with his Glock and he shot Vincent in the head with it. I drew, aimed and killed faster than Clint Eastwood.

'VINCENT!' I screamed. I saw him stand there with a hole in his head as if nothing had happened. The bullet was pushed out of the hole by some magical force and fell on the ground. The hole was gone in less than a second.

'What?' he said.

'That Kings of the bronze age thing is bullshit am I right?'

'Not entirely. I'll tell you later,' he said. He walked up the terrace and said: 'WOW!' as he held up the body. The bullet had gone straight through his left eye. Vincent and Doggio did the same thing to the body of Tygo. Vincent started howling when he had drunk Tygo dry. 'WHOOOO! THIS IS ME! THIS IS IT! WHOOOO! YES! JESUS MOTHERFUCKING PUSSY CUNT DONKEYFUCKER! I'VE NEVER BEEN SO ALIVE IN MY LIFE!' and he kept on howling. Then he calmed down a little and placed Tygo's head next to Ann's on the table.

'It makes me sad to look at this,' I said.

'It makes me sad too! Sad beyond believe! All this violence! If only we could learn to live without it....'

'It makes me sad because I wanted to hunt them. Now I can't hunt them anymore.'

Vincent looked at the heads. He went to the kitchen and came back. He sat before me with wide eyes and a quivering voice that said: 'I think I can do the most creepy and romantic thing in the universe for you if you have an open mind. I mean, not like them of course but...'

'What is it?'

'Brain surgery.'

'You mean... you mean you're going to build a Frankenstein out of Tygo and Annabel simply so I can hunt it?'

main light I could observe I needed to stand up my nose.

I quit perusing at that line. 'I know what its identity is,' I said.

'You will let me know it's a person obviously.'

'No, it's Susy, she's the school's cokewhore.'

'All things considered, no one says cokewhores can't be werewolves. Peruse on.'

Each time I put my father's firearm in my mouth and sit in the dimness, an inclination that sometime someone will remove me from here and assists me with carrying on with a daily routine worth experiencing prevents me from pulling the trigger and assist me god it with willing not be that fucking "boyfriend" of mine. He deals with me like trash and even beats me some of the time yet he's exceptionally manipulative and he keeps me snared on the numbskull.

I was trusting possibly you would remove me from here, in light of the fact that I discovered what you are. I'm pretty freaking guileless Vincent, yet I never believed that Twilight bologna planned to save me. However, no doubt, during

lunch, I followed you to your vehicle the principal day you
were at school and I saw you change and drink blood.

I love you Vincent, and in the event that you don't adore
me, if you don't mind, kindly kill me and drink my blood
since I can't change without you and I can't continue to put
in any amount of work. I would much prefer pass on as
your vampire food than continue to live as Tygo's sperm
pail.

My heart is yours, as is the blood it is siphoning,

Susy

Kindly call me, my number is on the back.

'Jesus,' Vincent said.

'That is the saddest thing I at any point read.'

'Better believe it, it's truly tragic.'

I put the letters in my pocket and we just took a gander at
the street, considering how tragic it was.

After we drove out of the backwoods and were moving
toward town, I considered something. 'You said werewolves
change since they need to kill individuals out of frantic love,
right?'

'Indeed.'

'Anyway, consider the possibility that Tygo discovered Susy is enamored with you. Would that not be a justification behind him to turn assuming he was a werewolf?'

'You're correct Sam,' Vincent said without precedent for this story.

'Along these lines, presently we have four suspects.'

'It seems like it, yes.'

'For what reason do you need to be so amazingly charming!' I said and I punched him on the shoulder. He chuckled, 'Would you say you were actually a chess champion in Denmark?'

'Jed var Danmarks bedste,' he said as he drove the vehicle into the parking area and got the wheelchair out of the storage compartment, 'I believe we're on schedule for math,' he said, 'I really look at the timetable. We both have math.'

'Why of school Vince? We as of now have their numbers and dislike they aren't ready to come to you. Simply advise Susy to bring her beau along so you can show him something new and we'll discover who it is at your place. How would you discover really?'

'You look at them without flinching and you can check whether they lie when you ask them. Likewise, you can taste it yet you need to drink a great deal. What's more I won't show that sweetheart of hers something new. I will kill him however, notwithstanding on the off chance that he is a werewolf or not.'

'I might want to see that Vincent, yet would we be able to please not go to fucking math?'

'Okay Sam. We can simply go to my place to Netflix and chill meanwhile. I have a beamer,' he said and he set the wheelchair back in the storage compartment and drove off the parking area.

'Vince?' I said as we crashed out into the road.

'What is it Sammie?'

'I need to let you know something.'

'What is it Sammie?'

'I never watched Twilight.'

'You haven't missed a lot.'

'Vince?'

'Is that right?'

'Will you watch Twilight with me?'

'Okay Sammie. We've experienced a ton however I think this will be our most prominent experience yet.'

'I suspect as much as well,' I said and I thought, 'Poor Susy.' and afterward I thought, 'Except if she's a werewolf.'

We were unable to move beyond the initial ten minutes of Twilight so we just screwed on the love seat. I was unable to accept the straightforwardness with which he had conveyed me up that large number of steps. After a fast contention we concluded that assuming it was Lemmy's child I was conveying that some weed won't hurt it thus we got high, then, at that point, we screwed again on the porch outside and stayed there for some time peacefully. 'I will call them,' Vincent said at last. For removed his telephone from his pocket and set it on speaker.

'Hi?'

'Annabel?'

'Who are you?'

'Vincent. I got your letter.'

'Vincent... Where could you have been? Also the thing would you say you will do?'

'I will welcome you over for supper this evening. We can discuss it. Wear something attractive and tasteful. There will be more visitor.'

'Who are they?'

'You'll see.'

'Could it be said that they are rich?'

'Indeed.'

'How late?'

'The evening gathering is from seven till twelve at my home, then, at that point, we'll choose if we need to transform it into one more sort of party.'

'Okay. I'll be there,' she said and she made two kiss commotions and was going to hang up however Vincent said: 'Stand by!' and Ann expressed: 'What is it?'

'Something vital. Assuming you intend to bring wine, I like red.'

'Okay Vincent,' she said and afterward Vincent hung up the telephone. I grinned.

'Alright, next suspect.'

'I want a smoke first,' Vincent said and he lit a cigarette. He dilled the number. We held up five seconds to that blare, before it went over.

'Please...' said a voice on the opposite side of the telephone.

'It's Vincent Susy.'

'I'm... I'm... O my God.... I was going to... O my God...'

'Where could you Susy be?'

'At... I'm at the old scaffold Vincent.'

'Jesus. I'll get you. Simply wait and do nothing insane OK?'

'OK...' Susy said and she began crying.

'I'll be there in a short time,' Vincent said and he hung up the telephone. After Vincent left, I removed my telephone from my pocket and planned and requested my sentiment top thing.

Furthermore similarly as that was done, Ann strolled into the house. 'Why are you here Sam?' she inquired.

'Why are you here? The party is at seven, didn't you hear?'

'No doubt, however why are you here?'

'I'm getting dead.'

'You're peculiar. Where's Vincent. I need to assist him with the arrangements. An evening gathering is better all the time with a young lady's contact I say. Beneficial thing I came cuz you don't seem as though you could be of much assistance. I heard your father's gay. What's more that he is in a state of insensibility or something to that effect. What is it Sam? For what reason do you see me like that?'

'I simply have PMS Annabel, don't stress over it.'

'At any rate, look what I brought: Vincent wine!' she said and she held a red container of Vincent wine in the air. 'It's truly costly. Beneficial thing I have a few class and have any familiarity with these things,' she said as Vincent strolled in the house with Susy, who had a bruised eye and a cut on her eyebrow.

'Vincent! There you are. What befell you Susy?' Ann inquired.

'I become inebriated with Tygo the previous evening and I fell against the latrine when I needed to upchuck. Then, at that point, I needed to regurgitation and I woke up in my blood and regurgitation.'

'You shouldn't drink so much Susy, you're now awkward enough when you're calm.'

Vincent's eyes became red and his teeth began showing up.

'O.M.G.' Ann said, 'this is very much like Twilight!'

'It's actually in no way like in the motion pictures.' I said and afterward Vincent bit her head off in one nibble. He drank every last bit of her blood directly from her neck as he held up her headless body as though it was a Coca Cola. She was depleted and blue in under ten seconds. He tossed the headless blue bitch at Doggio and Doggio processed her even faster than Vincent had depleted her blood. Her breaking bones were the best music I had at any point had the delight of paying attention to with the exception of Motörhead. For set her head on the table. 'Call Tygo and welcome him over for an evening gathering,' he told Susy, 'I think the moon is full this evening!' And he checked out me with the most unnerving smile that a flood of blood at any point spilled out of. 'Not terrible,' he told me, 'for a B-negative I mean.'

'Can... would you be able to get it done?' she said as she gave her telephone to Vincent. She was shaking everywhere. It helped me to remember the melody Shaking everywhere.

'Give me the telephone Susy. I'll call Tygo.' I said and Susy gave me the telephone. It was at that point going over.

'Howdy Tygo, it's Sam.'

'Howdy sugar, why you callin' me on my young ladies' phone?'

'I'm getting high in the backwoods with Susy however she dropped. I think Vincent was additionally here a little while ago. We truly need some Angel Dust and a dick that is somewhat greater than five inches. We're at Vincent's place. Everyone appears to know where that is for reasons unknown not terrible, but not great either would it be advisable for you. You going to be there?'

'Better believe it... Imma be there. How much residue you want?'

'The amount you got?'

'Beyond what you can ever exertion biatch so let me know what you really want.'

'Five grams.'

'That is a hundo darling. You got a hundo?'

'I got a hundo. Would you be able to be there down the middle?'

'Child I be there in TEN! Get that pussy wet for me will ya?'

'You get that pussy wet yourself Tygo.'

'Ayt. I'm coming back from Denver, I can be there in ten,' he said and he hung up the telephone.

'Okay,' Vincent said, 'Susy would you be able to sit tight in the kitchen for five minutes? There are a few private things Sam and me need to talk about.'

Susy cried delicately and left the family room without a word.

'I don't think Ann is the werewolf. She didn't taste any unique in relation to the following B-negative bitch in the line for the restroom. Presently I will kill Tygo and on the off chance that I don't taste any in his blood you know what we need to do right?' he murmured.

'Jesus Vincent,' I murmured back, 'You don't figure Susy would do that isn't that right?'

'Individuals are convoluted Sam. The one thing I gained from concentrating on cerebrums is that you can never get them.'

'Okay, however would I be able to ask you a certain something?'

'What is it?'

'Would I be able to if it's not too much trouble, be the one that kill

'I could attempt Sam... I could attempt... It will be the most confounded activity of all time. I'd need to call my dad. It will take every last bit of me. Be that as it may, I want to get it done. The bodies are still new. In any case, I need to begin right now you hear me. Right now.'

'That would be superb Vincent yet I don't get, what cerebrum would you place in there? They generally had chance through the head!'

'Indeed, yet Tygo through the left eye and Ann through the right eye!'

'What of it?'

'Don't you know this? You have two cerebrums! I will make kid young lady cerebrum out of Tygo and Ann, interface the sides of the equator and put it in Susy's mind!'

'Furthermore you will do that here on the kitchen table?'

'No, are you frantic?' he said as he put the foot stool in the corner and moved up the floor covering that was under there. 'I'll do it in my research facility!'

'You have a research center?! That is so fucking cool...'

'I'll show you later,' he said as he conveyed Ann's and Tygo's heads down the steps under the weighty metal lids. 'In any case, until further notice, it's significant not to go there regardless,' his voice reverberated from beneath. 'You simply need to deal with me since I really want all my concentration and energy in carrying this activity to a fruitful closure.'

'For what reason is it so cold down there?' I asked on the grounds that a chilling freeze came up from the opening.

'With the goal that the cerebrums don't spoil.'

'What minds?'

'Of the canines.'

'What canines?'

'How treat think I need to rehearse on? I go to pounds and take on canines who would have been put down in any case so in some measure now they can be great for science. Try not to ask me poop this evening. Simply keep yourself engaged and make me supper any other way I'll always be unable.'

'In any case, my leg is broken!'

'Okay, request pizza then, at that point. You can take the thing off tomorrow as indicated by Waking Dove and in three days you can run. I'll ensure Frankenstygann is finished by then, at that point. See, on the off chance that you don't need me to do this... I'm doing this for you Sam.'

'You're additionally doing it for yourself. Also Frankenstygann sounds moronic.'

'I'm doing it for ourselves and Frankenstygann is the coolest fucking name of all time! Be that as it may, it's your petition play with so you can name it in the event that you need however it sure won't be cooler than Frankenstygann!'

'Okay Vincent. Do it then, at that point. Furthermore I will name this delightful supplicate of mine...' I said and I began giggling yet I put my hand before my mouth since it was only the most exceedingly awful joke I've heard.

'How treat call it?'

'It's downright terrible yet it's truly entertaining.'

'TELL ME!'

'You're not Jewish, right?'

'No, why?'

'ANN FRANKENSTEIN!'

'Indeed! Above all, REQUIEM!' he said as he left his underground research facility and he tapped the I-cushion. It made Mozart's memorial reverberation full volume out of the opening. He got the container of Vincent wine, took a taste and conveyed Susy's body and the jug down to his insane lab rat vampire prison. I thought, 'to hell with it', and I lit a smoke. I chose to keep it at that. I just paid attention to the clamors that came from the research facility. Sawing clamors and blaring gadgets, and here and there boisterous chuckles and reviles from Vincent. It continued for quite a long time before he emerged from there.

'Espresso time,' he said, 'You want to espresso?'

'Just put me in bed,' I said. He took me off the lounge chair and put me in his bed.

'Please accept my apologies however I don't have the opportunity to give you a sleep time story.'

'The main sleep time story I care about is on my butt.'

'I can in any case taste the werewolf in Tygo's blood. I never felt so invigorated... I never had such a lot of energy. What's more I will do the most...'

'Show me my butt Vincent!' I said. Vincent turned me around and left the room. He returned quickly with a little hand reflect in his grasp, through which I could see my butt in the enormous mirror toward the side of the room. He lifted my skirt up and pulled my underwear down. Then, at that point, he ripped the swathe off. 'Nibble me.' it said in little and exquisite letters. He tapped my butt delicately, kissed my cheek and left the room without a word.

I observed Ghargatron's letter in my pocket and the late evening sun that avoid through the draperies furnished me

with enough light to understand it. I read that puzzle again
and again. It was gradually getting dull. I heard Mozart
transform into Motörhead sooner or later and afterward I
heard Motörhead transform into Britney Spears. I
continued to consider it. Every one of the mixes went
through my head. Then, at that point, I murmured it with a
shaking voice in the dimness: 'Aha... aha... it's so self-
evident... he left at 3:36. I'm a math genius!'

Stunned was heard. I addressed my telephone. 'Greetings
Sam, happy you got. It's Buck. It's not as yet dull but rather
Vincent said he would bring you back at sunset and it's
arriving. Is it true or not that you are coming?'

'I planned to call you. I went to the specialist and he let me
know I'm not pregnant. He likewise took the coffin off. I'm
at Vincent's home in the forest at this point. I need to
remain there for a few days. Get my head fixed in the
outside air. That is okay isn't it?'

'Where does he reside?'

'On the finish of the eighth back road on the avoided when
you drive south with regard to town.'

'Alright, I'll stop by tomorrow.'

'I couldn't say whether that will be helpful Buck I...'

'I'll come over the present moment.'

'Buck, kindly don't, things are a little...'

'O, I comprehend, I'll come around tomorrow in the late evening so you'll have the opportunity to tidy up from the party.'

'That would be fine Buck,' I said and I recently trusted that Vincent would be finished with his activity by then, at that point. I was unable to hold on to chase Ann Frankenstein. I contemplated what sort of rifle I needed to utilize. 'Four days until Christmas,' I said, petting my leg, and dreaming about the chase, pursuing Ann Frankenstein with Doggio close by, I rested the most brilliant rest. At the point when I woke up, I thought 'Crap. What was it once more?' and rapidly I recalled that it was 3:36. I hollered 'Vincent!' and Vincent didn't come. However, Waking Dove said I could take the coffin off today and that I could stroll at this point so I got up and left the room.

There were all the while hacking and sawing commotions from underneath the house yet Vincent was lying on the couch with earphones on, out of which the melody Everytime was heard stopped noisily. On the ground were five void jugs of red wine and an unfilled segment of those morphine pills lay on the table close to a debris train filled over the top with joint butts. I chose to simply allow him to rest yet I pondered who was hacking and sawing Ann Frankenstein together down there. I got to the kitchen and cut that coffin off with a steak-blade, then, at that point, I eliminated the rope, which took me around two hours since that rope was tight around there in an exceptionally convoluted manner.

Exactly when that was done, I heard it coming from the research center, that old, old cry each crazy lab rat longs for:

'IT'S ALIVE! IT'S ALIVE! IT'S ALIVE AND IT WANTS TO HAVE SEX WITH ME!'

I remained on my leg and it appeared all good, somewhat more vulnerable than the right one however it didn't do any harm. I removed Vincent's earphones, switched off Everytime (it was by all accounts playing in a circle) and chose to keep an eye on Ann Frankenstein. 'Screw ME OLD MAN! Screw ME HARD! If it's not too much trouble! I'LL SUCK YOUR DICK!'

There was a tent in a huge white room with a wide range of PC things and machines on the divider. A chill went through my spine in light of the virus. I saw a few hazy spots through the thick plastic of the tent. I could make out the beast and a man that was sewing her head however I was unable to see his face. 'Vincent! Come in. We've done the best thing men has at any point done! We have made: the prostitute of the future!'

I made the way for the tent and saw an exceptionally elderly person with white hair standing out in a wide range of bearings. He was smoking a cigarette and sewing Ann Frankenstein's temple. She looked similarly as excellent as Susy did before she passed on. With her dazzling blue eyes, dark hair and blushing cheeks. 'Who are you?' the man asked as he gazed upward.

'Sam I am, Vincent's better half.'

'Please to meet you. See this marvel of science,' he said as Susy, I mean Ann Frankenstein admired me. Her eyes were wide and her voice was temperamental. 'Sit on my prostitute face Sam! I'll suck your twat! Piss all around my

fucking prostitute face Sam! If it's not too much trouble...
I'll lick your butt sphincter... I'll do anything...'

'Quiet down Ann Frankenstein!' I said and she recently
began breathing vigorously in the middle of licking her lips.
'Thus, who are you?' I inquired.

'I'm Ludwig Offenbach, Vincent's dad. I was doing a little
mind a medical procedure masterclass in the college of
Grand Junction whenever my kid called me about a chance
to do the most muddled cerebrum medical procedure
activity at any point done. At the point when I showed up
sooner than expected toward the beginning of today,
Vincent was on the finish of his ropes. It takes a great deal
of a man to do a thing like this. Be that as it may, he had
effectively done the majority of the work and he just passed
on the subtleties to me so he could at long last become
inebriated. Yet, presently it's done so I can get tipsy as well,
and afterward I will screw the skank of things to come!'

'AHHH! Indeed!' Ann Frankenstein shouted altogether
sexual craziness.

'Wouldn't that be somewhat dishonest?'

'Better believe it... both of you are actually the power with
regards to morals in medication would you confirm or deny
that you are? Do nothing to Ann Frankenstein OK, don't
contact her. We want the mind to settle first.'

'Will she act somewhat more ordinary after you do that?'

'Who can say for sure. We've never seen a kid/young lady cerebrum previously so we have no clue about the thing it will do.'

'Alright,' I said and I just strolled after Ludwig to the front room. Ludwig got a rucksack off one of the seats and hauled a jug of vodka out of it. He drank 33% of the container in one swallow and afterward he lit another cigarette. 'I will play some Liszt on the piano if it's all the same to you. I generally become inebriated after an activity and play Liszt, until I

'Well, tough luck Rick, you'll have to find another Morty to do that shit for you.'

'What are you talking about? My name is Ludwig. And this is for science. Come one, you'll like it. Vincent would want you to. I know you women are all just as slutty as that creature below. It's just that the right hemisphere is preventing you to act on it but now that that is replaced by its male counterpart you get the slut of the future! I mean, sure my son must love you but you have to understand that he'll leave you for Ann Frankenstein the very day you stop sucking his dick,' he said. I got the 42 out of my ankle holster and shot him in the balls. He screamed and fell to the floor. Vincent woke up.

'What the fuck... what the fuck is this shit... what's that?' he said as he put his hand on his forehead. 'Was that Ann Frank? WOW! What the fuck! Sam did you just shoot my dad's balls off?'

'He was gonna... he was going to fuck Ann Frank!'

'What? That is fucking disturbing dad!'

'What do you know?!' Ludwig screamed in agony, holding the wound where once his balls were, *'She is the slut of the future!'*

'She was supposed to be a pray. I fine-tuned the brain. She was supposed to be terrified. Not horny.'

'Those two things aren't far apart... fucking Christ... fucking bitch... I... ARG... I didn't mean to...'

'Yes, you did you sexist bigot! You turned my beautiful Ann Frank into the slut of the future!' I said.

'Well... what do you think is more useful to society?'

'Shall I put this fucker out of his misery Vincent?' I asked as I pointed the gun at Ludwig's head.

'Jesus dad! All these years we've been doing brain surgery... Ever since mom died of that tumor and I thought... but these were your sick fucking intentions?'

'You don't understand! All the problems of the world are there because bitches aren't putting out. All the wars... this would have saved it... now can you please just fucking kill me already you stupid fucking bitch! I'll have to do it myself anyways now you made some sort of genderless abomination out of me!'

And just as I was about to pull the trigger Vincent said: 'WAIT.'

'Vince, I understand he's your father but...'

'NO SAM. It's just that I've got some Frankensteining to do,' he said as he pulled another bottle of vodka out of his dad´s backpack and dragged Ludwig down the hole by his collar. He was looking at me maniacally as he walked down the stairs and he took a big sip of the vodka.

'NO! DON'T FRANKENSTEIN ME! I'M YOUR FATHER! KILL ME VINCENT! I AM YOUR FATHER! KILL ME!' Ludwig was screaming as he was dragged into the laboratory.

'AW YES! Old man.... Did you come to fuck me? Please old man...' I heard Susy's voice say.

'He won't be fucking anybody anymore!' Vincent yelled as he walked up the stairs to closed the hatches. 'Get out of here Sam,' he said.

'I know the answer.'

'The answer to what?'

'Ghargatron's riddle.'

'What is it?'

'Not saying.'

'Why not?'

'Because I want to be the one opening the vault.'

'Are you one-hundred percent sure.'

'Yes.'

'Just give it to me and I will enter it in the vault. I would way rather be dead than to have to see you die.'

'And you don't think the same counts for me?'

'Alright. Let's go to the Gharnagan before someone beats us to the game then you crazy bitch. But if I get the riddle before we get there it is going to be *me* entering the code you understand?'

I nodded. 'Give me the gun,' he said and I gave him the gun. He went back into the laboratory. There was one shot and a scream of Ludwig where I hoped to hear two shots and no screams at all. He walked out, closed the hatch and said: 'Let's make a crazy rich bitch out of you!'

'RICH BITCH!' I screamed and Vincent shot the gun at the ceiling.

'RICH BITCH!' Vincent screamed and then we noticed it. The glass of the door was broken and Doggio sat calmly next to a gigantic pile of shit on the terrace with glass in his fur.

8, The Vault

'Vince, since I've missed so much schooling, can you school me?' I asked while Vincent was racing full throttle through the forest.

'Oh yeah... mythical history. Later on, baby. I have to think. I want to be the one that gets rich or dies trying.'

'You'll never get it.'

'I am Denmark's greatest chess player and the world's greatest brain-surgeon.'

'Well, I am Sam,' I said as his tires peeped when he drove up the road and away from town.

'Sam you am. But let me think now. Get me some Motörhead and speed. There's a pharmacy in the cupboard. It's the bag with the blue sticker.'

'You wanna snort it off my tit?'

'Sure, if you can hold your tit steady.'

I put Motörhead's *Bastards* (all the CD's were there now) in the stereo and speed on my tit. I could not hold my tit steady and the speed fell off as it was approaching Vincent's nose. 'Just give me the bag I'll do it off my knife,' Vincent said. I gave him the bag and he did that. He gave the silver knife and the bag back to me and I also sniffed some. I never did speed before but it sure seems to make life go a lot faster. After a long drive that seemed very short, he turned the car into a dirt road in the forest again and after a long and bumpy ride through that forest that also seemed very short Vincent stopped the car by a lake, on which a hydroplane was parked at a jetty.

'Is there really any need to get rich?' Vincent asked as he pointed at it, 'I already *am* rich.'

'I need to be more extravagant,' I said as we escaped the vehicle and into the plane. 'We have to fly low,' Vincent said as he started up the motor, 'underneath the radar.' and the plane began to drive itself over the water and lifted. As he was flying the thing pretty low above land, he murmured a wide range of numbers and reviles. 'I can't fucking track down it. Are you certain you have the right combination?'

'Indeed.'

'If you don't mind, kindly let me know then, at that point. I'll allow you to open the vault.'

'No, you won't,' I said and afterward he said 'Screw Sam.' and he began murmuring numbers and reviles once more. He wheezed some more speed and I checked out this incredible place where there is fresh chances to succeed and plausibility that was flying by under. 'One country under God,' I murmured. 'What's more he was never on your side.'

In no time, we were flying over the sea. I had gotten some rest.

'At last,' Vincent said, 'autopilot.'

'Have you gotten it yet?'

'Pay attention to me Sam. Assuming you're off-base with regards to it and bite the dust the principal thing I will do is drive a stake directly through my dark little heart so consider it. We can in any case turn around. We needn't bother with Ghargatron's enormous fortune. We have one another and that will forever be sufficient.'

'I envisioned all the time of being the most extravagant and most insane bitch known to mankind. One of these things I have achieved and I don't think the chance of getting the other thing will come back again very soon.'

'Okay, I've abandoned the puzzle. It's only another hour of water and we'll arrive. Presently this may be the last hour we spend together.'

'You need to screw me?'

'No, I need to make music with you.'

'Do you have a guitar on your plane?'

'All things considered yes. I saw on Metalocalypse how some person leaped out of a plane with a guitar and played while skydiving with an amp flying behind him. It appeared to be a decent birthday present. We could simply ski-plunge together while my father flies the plane I thought. When it's all said and done, your birthday is more than a week and I truly needed to accomplish something special.'

'How could you realize that?'

'Did you fail to remember you have a Facebook?'

'Who utilizes Facebook any longer?'

'I do. I'm forty,' he said as he got up from the seat and went into the rear of the plane. He returned with two marshal amps on batteries, a Gibson SG, an electrical violin and some printed music.

'This is a truly cool piece I made for violin and guitar. I planned to give it to you tomorrow so you could concentrate on it and afterward you discover that after a couple of training plunges, we can play it during a sky-jump. It isn't so much that convoluted it's...'

'I can't peruse music Vince.'

'Then, at that point, how could you learn it?'

'YouTube instructional exercises.'

'Poop. Presently we can't play.'

'For what reason don't we simply stick?'

'I can't do that. I want like, notes and stuff,' he said as he tragically examined front of him.

'Play four notes,' I said.

'Which ones?'

'Who cares?'

'I do.'

'Then, at that point, you pick them.'

'Okay,' he said and he played a F, a D, a B level and a C with a vibrato.

'That is lovely Vince!' I said, 'Simply continue to play that after I tune.'

Vincent quit playing and I turned the E up. We played the entire hour. The sky was everlasting over the water that we passed as was the music, that we played like heavenly messengers, flying through it, however as I said, and I should rehash it, we would never endure. What's more there was the oil big hauler. Enormous astonishment: the Gharnagan was painted gold. Before it were hydroplanes stopped of a wide range of tones.

'Poop,' I said.

'Sit back and relax. They're likely not here for the puzzle.'

'Then, at that point, what are they here for?'

'To watch individuals get rich or pass on attempting.'

'I'll make m' all see... I'll make m' see what geeky timid Sam is able to do! What geeky Sam can get! What's more that is everything... I need everything... what's more I'll get it... or on the other hand I'll pass on trying.'

'I disdain you most for the things I love you for.'

'Same thing here,' I said as Vincent stopped his hydroplane before the Gharnagan. There was a drifting wharf with steps that went up to the deck. I heard extremely peculiar music play from over the deck. On the deck was a party going. In the boat was a tremendous pool and wherever around it were natural product trees and pot plants planted. Individuals in affair dresses and tuxedos were strolling in the middle of the plants, drinking blood out of champagne glasses and smoking and talking apprehensively in the peculiar, delicate music that appeared to appear unexpectedly. A kid in a dark tuxedo moved toward us.

'Ok Vincent! That should be that Sam you filled me in about.' He held his palm up and I put my hand in there. He kissed it delicately and said 'I'm Fredrich. Vincent and me have been companions for quite a long time. I was the one that persuaded my dad to turn him at age thirteen. You're not actually dressed for the passing party...'

'We are the passing party.' I said.

'Might it be said that you are going to? Do you know the conundrum Vincent?' he said as he held him by the shoulders.

'No, yet she does.'

'Vince... you're not going to let her... not her...'

'I trust her.'

'Jesus...' Fredrich said.

'No,' I said, 'Barabbas.'

'I'll get Kharkanov then, at that point,' he said as a tremendous screen illuminated on the scaffold and a voice was heard: 'Candidate number one is moving toward the entryway of the vault!' the voice said. A man in a green robe, who was smoking a line was seen strolling through a foyer. His hair was long, style and white. Then, at that point, the entryway of the vault was seen. It was gigantic. There was an opening in it with a major green button close to it. The button had a dollar sign on it. 'Offer ME A HAND' the hint over the opening read. Close to the sign was a scoreboard put. The man enjoyed a drag from his line and tranquilly put his hand in the opening. There was something locking it. A tick. The man accomplished something with his arm and the main number of the scoreboard began evolving. He halted at six and squeezed the button. 'Indeed,' I said. The number began flickering. Then, at that point, it became red and the man in the green robe was shocked on the spot. He was nothing however dark remains in a have much of any significance of seconds.

'That is so freaking metal,' Vincent said.

'Indeed,' I said.

'I'm Kharkanov,' an exceptionally old looking person of color in an earthy colored robe said, 'I assume you realize I am the dad of Ghargatron. I heard from Fredrich that you needed to endeavor breaking the safe. I will take you to the vault.'

'Come on Sam,' Vincent said, 'we should go to the vault together.'

'Indeed how about we go together.'

Kharkanov showed us the way to the corridor and wished us best of luck. Under humming TL lights and cameras, we strolled through the long foyer. There was the entryway. There was the opening. I stack my hand in the opening and felt four pins against my arm, pushing down on it not hard enough for my arm to drain. I felt a handle on the finish of the opening.

'Stand by Sam' Vincent said, 'I'll give you a hand.'

'But you'll be electrocuted to Vince!'

'Let's get rich or die trying... *together*,' he said and I gave him my hand.

I played around with the knob again until I had the number six as the first digit.

'Alright Vince. Press the button.'

'Stop fucking with me Sam!'

'I don't really know absolutely sure but whatever,' I said and turned it to three. Vince pressed the button without a word and he didn't let go of my hand.

'And this was like... five? I thought five... Maybe four... No definitely one. Yeah, I think it's definitely one. Wait! This one IS six. Pres it Vincent.'

'Do you THINK it is...'

'I just remembered it was three.'

'Are you sure?'

'Just press the fucking button you pussy,' I said and Vincent pressed the button. Again, the number turned green after blinking for two seconds.

'You're fucking with me, right?'

'Maybe I am and maybe I'm not. Maybe I just don't give a fuck. Maybe I just found a free lottery ticket and I'm feeling a little too lucky.'

'Can you PLEASE stop fucking with my head!'

'Alright, but you have to promise me something...'

'What is it Sam? Anything...'

'You're going to have to taste your dick on my mouth in the morning every day before breakfast and sport-life.'

Vincent closed his eyes and sighed. 'Alright Sam,' he said, 'Just please stop fucking with me.'

I quickly entered the next number 'Press,' I said and the door went open. A large, square metal cube was behind it and in that cube, we saw the following:

A very large painting of Ghargatron, with the president's wife Melody Triumph, naked, in all her beauty on a leash, crouching before him. Doggio was wearing his crown and was standing next to him on his rear paws. Ghargatron wore the biggest grin of two rows of the whitest teeth in the blackest face and in between those teeth was held, an immense blunt that was a foot long and two inches in dynamiter. It covered the middle of the entire back wall of the vault. Strangely enough, there was no golden frame around the picture but just a humble wooden one.

In the one corner of the vault next to the painting was a cube of over a hundred-thousand white bags of what I presumed to be cocaine. It was stacked to the ceiling. In the other corner was a similar stack of a brown substance that I presumed to be heroin, also stacked to the ceiling. In the other corners were cubes of the same size. One of which was built out of bricks of gold and the other was build out of dollar bills, held together with rubber bands. And in the middle of these stacks was parked: a Bugatti, and I had never seen a pinker thing. Everything about the car was painted in the pinkest pink except for the rims, those were baby blue. 'Jesus,' I said and I walked to the dollar stack to find out they were all five-hundred-dollar bills. 'How did he get all this?' I asked Vincent.

'Who cares,' he said, 'You have it now!'

'*We* have it now,' I said as Vincent opened the Bugatti.

'I found his will and a golden Magnum Python. Is that an ivory handle? Sweet.'

'You want to do the honors Vincent?'

'I shall do the honors.' Vincent said and he started reading.

I, Ghargatron, shall, in the event of my imminent death, bestow all I possess to my dog; Doggio, and that includes my title. Doggio shall now be the King of Kings! I have found no other creature that is worthy. I saw it in his eyes. He must be crowned in three days after this will is read.

I was told by my good friend Offenbach of the song of "King of Kings", by the musical ensemble Motörhead. 'Yeah?' I said and It instantly became my very favorite musical piece ever created. I stated clearly that there is no more need to produce or listen to any other music and after I heard it, I repeated that statement. After this will is read it shall be the new anthem of Ghargatronia, the floating land over which Doggio now rules and when the song is opened by the phrase "BEHOLD THE KING, THE KING OF KINGS!", and Doggio is seen, all that can hear it but the owner of Doggio must bow down before Doggio or lose their heads.

I shall bestow my dog; Doggio, to whoever has opened the vault.

Also, I know it is none of my business but I strongly advice my father to give his turn to whomever opened this vault. I have great hopes for that wise or obscenely lucky individual.

'You were right Vincent,' I said for the first time in this story.

'About what?'

'About Ghargatron being pretty crazy.'

'Yeah... I was pretty right about that. You want to get out of here?'

'Yeah. We better tell Doggio he's the king of Ghargatronia.'

'I think he'll be happy to hear it.' Vincent said. On the back door of the vault was a little pad on which you could enter a new combination. I knew that because of a sign that said; ''Always enter new combination before closing '', so I entered my first ever code, which was 123 and we closed the door of the vault. On the end of the hallway, Kharkanov was waiting.

'Do you have the will Vincent?'

'Yes.'

'She must go up to the bridge and read it to the proud people of the floating land of Ghargatronia.'

'OK,' I said.

'But she cannot go and read this will dressed like this, now can she?'

'I like green dresses,' I said and a little later I was standing on the bridge of the ship, dressed in a gorgeous green dress that fitted almost perfectly and had sparkles all over it. They even did my make-up. And I read the will to that crowd of vampires, dressed in gala dresses and tuxedos on that beautiful golden oil-tanker of my dreams; the Gharnagan. They all started cheering when that was done; 'DOGIO! DOGIO! DOGIO! OUR WISE KING HAS SPOKEN!'

Black flags with white bulls-eyes came from nowhere. Then they all started chanting: 'HAIL THE KING! THE KING OF KING!' and I asked Kharkanov if he would be so kind to play *King of Kings* full volume to really get the party going. He took his phone out of his pocket, tapped it a little and louder than ever heard before; Motörhead started playing. BEHOLD THE KING, THE KING OF KINGS!' sang Lemmy and as a picture of Doggio was shown on the screen, wearing Ghargatron's crown, everybody, even Vincent, got on their knees except for Kharkanov and nerdy little Sam.

On the flight back Vincent said: 'Sam, I've been thinking lately.'

'Oh shit.'

'What?'

'You mean you did all this shit and you only started thinking *lately* about what the fuck you're doing?'

'I want... I want...'

'What do you want Vincent? I have everything.'

'No, you have a dog that has everything. And I want to start a heavy-metal band with you.'

'That is so fucking cool Vince! We should totally do that!'

'And I've also been thinking that you should be the one that names it.'

'You already said it. It was the greatest name for a heavy-metal band in the history of history of history and even before that.'

'What is it? What did I say?'

'PUSSY CUNT DONKEYFUCKER!'

'Ghargatron would be so proud of you right now.'

'I know Vince, I know.'

'You know something about the floating land of Ghargatronia Sam?'

'No. Except for the fact that my dog is the king of it of course.'

'It's pretty much everywhere and it pretty much controls everything.'

'One nation under *dog*,' I said as we flew over the coast.

'I really wonder how this is going to work out.'

'You want a riddle you CAN solve?'

'Alright.'

'What does DOG spell backwards?'

'That's a good one. I'll have to think about it.'

'Yeah...'

'Sam?'

'What is it Vincie?'

'Can we please just call the band Pussy Cunt?'

'That's OK Vince, that's OK...'

Epilogue

After we walked up the stairs to the terrace leading up to Vincent's house, we found out that it wasn't there anymore. Everything was completely torn down. Only the heavy metal hatches of Vincent's Laboratory were still there. Doggio was lying on the terrace with a wound on his ribs. He was still breathing.

'God damn werewolves...' Vincent said.

'But who would fall in love with Doggio?' I asked. Doggio grunted in the blood. 'I mean... what *human* would fall in love with Doggio?' I said but Doggio just kept on grunting. 'I'm sorry for things I don't mean to say Doggio, King of Kings, for I know they are meaningless,' I said and then Doggio stopped grunting.

'Maybe it was someone who was in love with Ann Frankenstein,' Vincent suggested.

'Who may that be then, at that point?'

'My father.'

'Yet, I thought you shot him!'

'I just shot his kneecap so he was unable to go anyplace and afterward I took him out. After that I concluded that it would presumably be more secure to wrap some tie-folds over his wrists before I could get to Frankensteining the fuck out of him.'

'You need to see what's in there?'

Vincent flipped his blade up and I coaxed the firearm out of his holster.

'You better have silver shots in here.'

'That doesn't work. The silver is something momentary through which your energy needs to stream and it can't do that in the event that it's not associated with your skin while it contacts the werewolf.'

'You live you learn. How about you kill this fucker Vince?'

Vincent strolled into the research center. 'It's now dead! As is Buck, I think. Buck? O no his actually relaxing.'

I strolled in. Ann Frankenstein was gone however there lay Ronnie, half turned and wherever were pieces of hide and puddles of blood. Buck had his silver pizza-shaper in his grasp. Toward the side of the Laboratory lay Vincent's father, tight up and dropped. 'What the heck occurred here?' Vincent said.

'That is a question I can't tackle by the same token.'

Vincent got a glass of water from a sink toward the side of his research facility and tossed it in Buck's face. Buck opened his eyes wide and said:

'Mother lover!'

'What occurred here Buck?' I inquired.

'Get me the fuck out of here, get me twofold bourbon and a smoke and I'll fill you in regarding it yet not up to that point!' he said as he tranquilly left the Laboratory. 'Gracious,' he said, 'here's vodka, that is sufficient for me. Accumulate round kids and I'll let you know the brave story of what the heck occurred here,' he said as he plunked down on a portion of the rubble with the container and lit a smoke. We sat before him.

'Okay, so I said I would come here to see you and I did. However at that point I saw the glass was broken. Additionally, a major heap of poo that your canine was sitting close to. I felt that wrecked glass was most likely from the party however you can never be excessively cautious so I got out my pizza-shaper and went in. I saw some opening in the floor and I thought about what was happening in there so I went down there. Furthermore what I saw there! I saw some fucking horrifying presence! I saw some child having intercourse with some close up chick, while some draining old fart was kicking the bucket on the floor. Presently this mother lover that was fucking... something was going on to him. This multitude of hairs were outgrowing his back... So, I imagined that was both of you and that Vincent was a werewolf like in Twilight or some crap. Yet, when that mother lover moved off after I strolled in, he looked in no way like you. He was generally light and poop and he had an eyepatch and he checked out me with these huge fucking blue eyes that resembled ALL BLUE and he said "run" in some insane voice and I said "What the fuck have you done to my cousin you fucking horrifying presence of nature?!" and he said he was safeguarding your honor, that he has killed the King of Kings and that he planned to kill your vampire sweetheart. I didn't have a clue thus I advised him to get the fuck out this moment yet he approached me so I cut that mother lovers throat with my sixteen-karat mother loving pizza-shaper! I needed to leave there yet I slipped over the blood and I probably fallen on my head or something like that. There's blood on there however I don't realize whether or not that is mine. I can't taste the distinction. He, what the heck happened to your canine?'

'Thus, Ronnie is likewise a werewolf?' Vincent said, 'obviously, he was enamored with you Sam... also he... it's sort of presumptuous that I didn't think about that since I think back on it.'

'You can basically highly esteem being the most self-important individual on the planet and be presumptuous with regards to that I presume.'

'It never happens that there is a werewolf and presently there were two of the fuckers...'

'Did you at any point do cocaine Vincent?'

'Indeed. Shouldn't something be said about it?'

'All things considered, I've never done cocaine yet I've seen individuals on it and I feel that may very well clarify the flavor of Tygo's blood.'

'Your right Sam,' Vincent said for the second time in this story and afterward his telephone rang.

'Vincent. Indeed. Great,' he said and he set the telephone back in his pocket.

'What is it?'

'That was Kharkanov. He has accepted Ghargatron's recommendation.'

'Goodness, would you be able to turn my father so he right? He'll escape his trance like state and we'll all chase the wolf together!'

'Yet, I need to become old with you, not with your father... '

'I know however by what other method would I be able to be sure he will awaken.'

Vincent plunked somewhere around Doggio and investigated his eyes. 'You did great kid. What's more now we likewise realize that it's adequate to set screwed by a switching werewolf around to become one. We didn't realize that previously. How about we chase it all together, you, Sam and me... and Sam's father! Presently I don't have the foggiest idea about Sam's father yet to turn him rather than her, he should be a WOW! What the heck is that! WHAT IN THE...'

'How treat see Vincent?' I asked as I sat close to him and checked out Doggio's eyes. They looked like typical large earthy colored Rottweiler-Beelzebat-Wolfdog eyes to me.

'My God no!' he said.

'How treated see Vincent?!'

'Your father... uhm... he is in extraordinary peril. I need to go to the clinic now. I'll need to turn him now. I'll meet you here in three hours,' he said as he ran down the steps.

'Vincent!' I shouted.

'Indeed?'

'Watch out.'

He approached me, immediately kissed me on the mouth and ran down the steps. I saw his Lexus race over the street and vanish into the scene. Buck remained close to me. 'We should get the fuck out of here before that fucking werewolf returns,' he said.

'In any case, what might be said about Doggio?!'

'Okay. I'll convey Doggio,' Buck said as he attempted with all his power to take Doggio off the ground. 'We can't go anyplace. At whatever point that mother lover returns, I'll simply fucking cut it with my mother loving sixteen-karat mother loving pizza shaper!' he said as he got that thing out of his pocket again and held it in Ninja of some kind or another position.

I set down before Doggio and I investigated his eyes, trusting I could see something yet they remained something very similar. 'You're the King of Kings Doggio... furthermore you're my canine... furthermore you're the King of Kings...' I continued to murmur to him. 'We will chase Ann Frankenstein Doggio, werewolf or not...', and afterward I saw something. It was Vincent. He strolled into the clinic. I saw him offer something to a specialist, then, at

203

that point, he provided that specialist with a roll of cash and he strolled on. He strolled in my father's room. I hadn't seen him since the mishap and I would have rather not. He looked terrible, with a wide range of cylinders and wires connected to him. And afterward I saw Vince reassessing him and he nonchalantly left the emergency clinic. 'I see a vehicle!' Buck hollered.

'Then, at that point, it's presumably not a werewolf.' I said.

'How would you know?'

'Since they move quicker without them.'

'Perhaps it's for camouflage.'

'It's presumably not yet we need to shield Doggio, he is the King of Kings so prepare your pizza shaper!'

'Alright,' Buck said and he took his ninja position once more.

'Something isn't right with you is there Buck?'

'I can't feel dread.'

'Never?'

'No, never felt it. I didn't overemphasize it all things considered. I never truly got what dread is for.'

'Amusement I presume... be that as it may, my dad... I just saw Buck, in Doggio's eyes that Vince...' and similarly as I said that, he came strolling up the steps.

'I need to let you know something Sam. At the point when I got to the clinic to shield your father from what I found in Doggio's eyes, I heard that he had simply calmly kicked the bucket in a state of extreme lethargy,' Doggio was uttering a low strong when he said that. I saw a piece of wood on the ground that appeared to be sufficiently sharp. 'I have something special for you Vince,' I said.

'I don't need any longer shocks Sam.'

'You'll adore this one. Simply shut your eyes,' I said and Vincent said: 'alright' and he shut his eyes. What's more exactly when he did that, I got that stake and stuck it straight through his heart. His eyes shot open. 'Why?' was the principal thing he said and afterward he tumbled down straight on his back. I saw that his eyes were as yet open and he was breathing intensely.

'You killed my dad!' I cried.

'Please accept my apologies... I needed to... I saw him according to the canine and I was unable to leave him alone a vampire!'

'What difference would it make? Since he's gay?'

'You would rather not know Sam. However, it isn't so much that. You would rather not know!'

'I sort of do Vincent. I sort of do,' I said as I squirmed the stake in his heart.

'AAAHH! Poo! No.... you would rather not know... just... guarantee me you won't examine his eyes Sam! It's simply that... WE DON'T WANT HOMOSEXUAL VAMPIRES SAM!' I checked out Doggio and Doggio's eyes were sparkling a red gleam over me. He had gotten up and was staying there.

'Try not to LOOK INTO HIS EYES SAM! Try not to LOOK INTO HIS EYES!' I went to the canine and sat before him.

I saw my mother hanging over a headstone, she appeared as though she was getting screwed and appreciating it. Then, at that point, the film according to the canine zoomed out and I saw that my father, as a priest, was fucking my mother. Vincent was correct; I would have rather not see that. Be that as it may, I continued to look. He got off and given my mother a few coins. I saw my mother stroll through a middle age city. She strolled into a little wooden house. There was an exceptionally huge and furry man there. Then, at that point, I saw him fucking her. I saw a child being conceived. I saw the child grow up. I saw individuals tossing tomatoes at her as the baby strolled down the road. I saw my mother, wearing bumps, converse with my father as a priest again and I heard an extremely boisterous murmur in my mind, it was my mother's murmur: 'witch', was that word. The child developed and developed and afterward I saw that it was me. I saw them cut my eye out. I saw Mathilda shout yet I was unable to hear her. And afterward I saw it. 'No....' I murmured

THE END

* 9 7 9 8 4 0 5 8 6 8 7 9 0 *